THROUGH THE NIGHT
LIKE A SNAKE

THROUGH THE NIGHT LIKE A SNAKE

LATIN AMERICAN HORROR STORIES

CALICO

Through the Night Like a Snake is ninth in the Calico Series.

"Rabbits" was first published as "The Formative Experience"
in the *Southwest Review* (Volume 107.3, 2022).

"The House of Compassion" is published with permission from Other Press.

Two Lines Press
582 Market Street, Suite 700, San Francisco, CA 94104
www.twolinespress.com

ISBN: 978-1-949641-57-8 (matte edition)

Cover design by Crisis
Typesetting and interior design by Marie-Noëlle Hébert
Printed in the United States of America

Library of Congress Cataloging-in-Publication Data available upon request.

THIS BOOK WAS PUBLISHED WITH SUPPORT
FROM THE NATIONAL ENDOWMENT FOR THE ARTS

NATIONAL
ENDOWMENT for the ARTS
arts.gov

DESDE QUE LLEGAMOS,
DORMIMOS EN LA ESCUELA.

BONE
ANIMALS

TOMÁS DOWNEY
TRANSLATED BY SARAH MOSES

WE'VE BEEN SLEEPING AT THE SCHOOL SINCE WE GOT HERE. Señora Margarita didn't say anything at first. But this morning she asked us to go somewhere else. She said it was because of the boys, José and Fermín, that this was no way to live. Of course, I told her. We know that perfectly well. We've been moving from village to village for months now, unable to find shelter or work. Porfirio, offended, backed away from her, picked up our things, and went out to wait for me. Fermín followed him. I would have liked to tell Señora Margarita that I trust Porfirio, that he's the reason I left the city, that I'd follow him to the end of the world, but I know how she would have looked at me. So I smiled and nodded, took José to the bathroom, and bathed him in the sink.

Sometimes Porfirio finds work for a day, and that's why we haven't moved on. He's familiar with the different regions, knows where there's seasonal work, and says we're better off here than in the south. They're building a new road down to the village, but they only need workers when the gravel trucks pull in. When they don't, Porfirio makes sure to stick around the construction site. He watches the workers from a distance, and it's like he's waiting for one of them to fall into the gorge so he can run up to the foreman wearing the dead man's hard-hat and gloves.

I keep telling him that we should leave. I say that if you go after your luck, eventually you find it. He says he needs some time to think. That afternoon, a woman at the park tells us about this place, a shack surrounded by a bit of land overtaken by weeds. It doesn't belong to anybody, she tells us, and has been empty for a long time. It's hard to get to. Porfirio asks for directions, jots them down on a piece of paper. He looks at me with feverish eyes and smiles. He thinks he was right to have waited. José crawls between my legs and Fermín, who's crouched down, places twigs across a trail of ants that's coming and going. Red ants. Be careful, they bite, I tell him.

We set out early. Porfirio with our stuff and Fermín upright, a bag weighing him down, though he doesn't complain. I carry José in my arms. Descending into the valley is easy, but then we have to climb back up. Parts of the path have been swallowed by the undergrowth, and Porfirio clears the way with a machete. We leave the village behind, and when we turn to look at it from the hillside, it seems small and distant. I sweat and gasp for breath. I'm afraid we're going to get lost. But Porfirio always finds his way, as though he were following a scent.

The house is damp and full of insects, the floor packed dirt. I feel a bit sad when I see it. It's not the house, which is solid and much better than nothing, but maybe the darkening sky, and the insects we have to sweep out quickly before the light is gone. When Porfirio asks, I lie and tell him I'm happy. We have everything we need here, he says, and strokes my hair. Right, I say, silencing what I feel at the sight of neglect in every filthy nook and cranny, at the smell of mold, and the dark shadows cast by the trees in the thicket out back.

We hear a stream nearby. Porfirio goes to get water and leaves us on our own. I look around and tell myself that this is fine, that everything is fine. The house is a single room, just a roof over our heads, really. There's a table and a cabinet, the wood rotten. Outside, under some sheet metal, there's a place to make a fire.

We cover the windows with plastic so the rain won't get in. The roof leaks here and there, but some places stay dry. José is crying; he won't latch to my breast. The mosquitoes buzz around in the dark, and I start a fire in the corner of the house to get rid of them. I look José over in the light of the flames. He's broken out in a rash, and his eyes are swollen, almost out of their sockets. I'm scared, but Porfirio says it's nothing, that José is just itchy. Fermín helps me spread our blankets on the floor.

I peel potatoes with Porfirio's knife and boil them. José is still crying. Porfirio leaves again; I don't know how he finds his way in the dark. If I so much as step away from the fire, I can't see my hands. He comes back with a minty herb, grinds it to a paste between two stones, and rubs it on José's rash. He stops crying right away. I ask Porfirio to show me how to make it.

I sleep badly and get up at dawn to clean. We pull out the weeds growing inside the house. In a corner, lying in the dirt, there's a small, carved animal, almost hidden, it seems. It's a big cat. Later I find a piranha and am amazed by its teeth. They're so small and detailed they could only have been carved by an impossibly skilled hand. Porfirio looks at them like he's entranced. We could sell them when we're in the village, I say. They might be worth something. He shakes his head, holding them in his hands like delicate objects. Afterward, he places the animals in a corner, arranging them carefully, one next to the other. It's only then, by the light of the fire, that they give off an opaque, white glint, and I realize they're made of bone. Uneasy, I turn away so I don't have to look at them.

I drag the rotting furniture outside and chop it up with an axe for kindling. Porfirio and Fermín dig a channel to divert the stream. There's so much to do it's overwhelming. But as long as I don't stop, there's no time to think.

In the afternoon, the boys fall asleep and we go for a walk. Porfirio leads me along a path heading north and shows me different herbs. There are herbs for cramps, headaches, fevers, others to help with digestion. You can take the pulp of this one fleshy leaf and make a poultice to spread over a cut. We find a guava tree along the path and eat until our stomachs swell, our mouths sweet and tart. We laugh like drunks. Porfirio kisses me and we lie down in the shade. I wish we could stay here, but soon it's time to get back.

The channel now reaches the house and forms a pool. We filter the water with stones then boil it. Even still, it's filthy water that tastes like dirt and dead bugs.

At night, Porfirio gropes around for me in the dark. It's as though he doesn't know which part of me he's touching, and I hold in my laughter. He breathes on the back of my neck, then lifts my skirt. I feel him pulsing between my legs, and when he comes, I push him out. He kisses me and strokes my cheek. He likes to look at me. I see the crystalline gaze I fell for. His eyes are like clear lagoons; you can see to the depths of them. Everything's going to be all right, I think.

Porfirio comes in from out back, sweating, his skin burned by the sun. He's carrying two birds he caught somewhere.

They're black, with hooked beaks and long legs. They were lame, he says, I don't think they could fly. The thought of eating them makes me squeamish—I don't even know what kind of birds they are. But going hungry is worse. We defeather them together, then gut them. The meat is tough and gray, but it's edible.

We work until the sun sets. Then we go inside to get away from the mosquitoes. This is the time of day I like best, the four of us together under our roof. I rub Porfirio's neck and shoulders with the herb he used on José—he says it cools him down. His skin is hot and swollen, his muscles tight. Porfirio is a strong man, and I love him. Fermín takes seeds out of the cloth they're wrapped in and looks at them curiously. I show him which ones are corn and tell him the big one is avocado, the brown ones cocoa.

Porfirio works the land; he's focused and takes his time. But the tomatoes need to be sown now; we have to hurry up. I go for a walk to explore and get an idea of where we are. Upstream there are banana and papaya trees. The soil is good; there's an abundance of fruit. I return carrying a heavy load in my dress and see Porfirio standing still, his back turned to me. He's holding the rake in one hand, his eyes focused on the ground. I walk over to him. Something white is sticking out of the earth. He bends down to pick it up and, very carefully, brushes the dirt off with his hand. It's a tiny owl, perfect just like the others.

That night I can't sleep. I keep waking up and sense that his eyes are open. He gets out of bed early and leaves to clear the land. He pulls up small tufts of weeds and rakes so slowly it's almost like he's not moving. It irritates me, but I need to be patient like he is.

There are several animals now: a scorpion, a lizard, a vulture. I ask Porfirio what we're going to do. I don't want them in the house. Moonlight comes in through the window at night, and when I wake in the early hours, I see them there, gleaming. What are you waiting for? I ask. We have to sow the seeds tomorrow, the earth only gives when it receives: those are your words. He looks at me silently. Then he goes back to what he was doing. He's using a dry weed like a brush, removing the earth from the animal he just found.

When there's a new one, Porfirio leaves it on a plank for Fermín, who removes the caked earth with his small hands. I've never seen him concentrate so hard. I can't watch the two of them anymore and leave to hunt whatever I can find—birds, lizards. We can't live off fruit alone. I take José with me. We follow the stream down to where the river begins. It's an hour on foot. The river is wide and strong, and at one spot the water overflows the banks, forming a pond. There are piranhas in it.

I see them when they catch their prey, a seething mass below the surface.

Porfirio and the boys are asleep. I climb over them and approach the animals in the corner. There's a squirrel monkey, some fish I've never seen before, and a sand snake that frightens me more than all the others. Not because it's a snake but because it's so perfect. Who could have carved it? And how? It's a thin and sinuous line with stripes down its back. And its eyes—its eyes are unbelievable.

The next morning, I lose my patience and yell at Porfirio. I tell him to throw the animals away, to get them out of our house. I don't want them under our roof. Will you at least talk to me? I ask. Look me in the eye and say something. He raises his head slowly; it's eerie how he's been moving these past few days, as though there's no need to hurry. No, he says. In due time.

José is running a fever, and Porfirio spends the day raking. I need to get to the village, but I don't know what to do about José. It's too hot to take him, and I can't leave him here alone. Fermín isn't talking to me now either. He spends his days with his father, removing earth from the animals, blowing on them, cleaning them until the last speck of dirt is gone. I bundle José up so he'll sweat and force him to drink herbal tea. He doesn't improve.

I'm awoken by a sound in the middle of the night. Porfirio is grinding his teeth. I see his tense jaw and that movement he makes, like he's biting down on something, bone on bone. José is burning up, his mouth swollen. I shake Porfirio, tell him his son is sick. He opens his eyes and looks at me as though he were very far away. Tomorrow, he says, and goes back to sleep.

The sun comes in through the window of the silent house. José is dead in my arms. I know this without even looking at him. I hold him to me as I weep, hear Porfirio rise and come closer. I can feel him take José from me, but I keep my eyes closed. I get up and follow him out back, where there's an open grave. I ask him when he dug it, but he refuses to look at me. Carefully, he places our boy in it. No, I say, as he begins to fill in the grave. I tell him to stop and fall to my knees. Fermín helps his father.

The days pass like dreams; I don't move or think. My knife is hidden among the blankets. Porfirio and Fermín are working out back; I hear them come and go, hear them breathing in their sleep. I don't know what they're doing—I don't want to know. They don't say a thing, and neither do I.

I need to get up and eat. What are they doing for food? I wonder. I'm weak but manage to find the guava tree, which is so full of fruit its branches are weighed down, almost to the ground. I eat four, five, and still don't feel full. I throw up.

At night, I wake wondering where the fantasy came from. How could I have believed the lie I told myself about Porfirio's clear gaze? How could I have followed him this far? He's always been a dark man who's never said much. A man who doesn't say what's on his mind is dangerous. I wake Fermín and tell him we're leaving. He rubs his eyes, stands up. But instead of coming to me he goes to his father and rouses him. Porfirio looks at me without moving, and I tell him I'm leaving. Neither of them says anything. I cry myself back to sleep.

In the morning I go down to the village. People look at me but don't recognize me. Maybe they don't remember me, or maybe I've changed too much. I've probably lost a lot of weight—I haven't looked at myself in a mirror in weeks. My clothes are dirty and torn. Across from the park there's a bus-load of tourists. The road down from the mountain is finished. I go up to the tourists to ask for money and many of them give me some, embarrassed by me or by themselves. I count the bills and coins and ask how much a ticket to the city costs. I have enough. I return to the house with soap and rice and tuck what's left among my belongings.

I bathe in the stream and see two of those birds that Porfirio caught when we first arrived. They look clumsy, poorly made. They flutter about on the ground without taking flight and when I approach them, they squawk hoarsely. I slice open the bigger one's throat with the knife. The other one looks at me blankly. When I approach, it takes a step back, stumbling like a drunk. I laugh to myself, among the trees and creatures.

I drag the birds to the house, clean them, and make a stew. I eat slowly, let my stomach settle. Later, I hear Fermín and Porfirio eating the leftovers.

The sun has just risen and I open my eyes. Fermín is looking at me, pointing outside. I get up, confused, and follow him. Porfirio is digging next to José's grave. I ask him what he's doing. His hands are in the earth, slowly moving it around. What is this? Answer me, I yell. He looks at me and lets the earth fall from his fingers, until a small horse carved of bone appears. The animal is beautiful, a foal with its head raised. I run a finger over its mane—it's so smooth it feels like hair—and I see that beyond Porfirio there are three open graves. Fermín is smiling and Porfirio's eyes seem transparent again. I don't know whether to cry, laugh, or scream.

THAT SUMMER

MARIANA ENRIQUEZ
TRANSLATED BY MEGAN MCDOWELL

LA CIUDAD ERA PEQUEÑA PERO NOS PARECÍA ENORME
SOBRE TODO POR LA CATEDRAL, MONUMENTAL Y OSCURA,
QUE GOBERNABA LA PLAZA COMO UN CUERVO GIGANTE.

IN THE
DARK

THE CITY WAS SMALL BUT IT SEEMED HUGE TO US, MOSTLY because of the cathedral, monumental and dark, that loomed over the plaza like a gigantic crow. Whenever we passed it, walking or in the car, my father would explain how its neo-Gothic style was unique in Latin America and that it was unfinished because it was missing two towers. It had been built on clayey, unstable ground that couldn't support the building's weight; its bricks were exposed, and it had a glorious but neglected look. A beautiful ruin. The most important building in our city was in constant danger of a cave-in, notwithstanding its Italian stained-glass windows and details carved from Norwegian wood. We used to sit in front of the cathedral on one of the benches in the plaza, and we'd watch for some sign of collapse. There wasn't much to do that summer. The weed we smoked, bought from a suspicious dealer who talked too much and called himself the Super, stank of pesticides and made us cough so hard we'd often get dizzy beside those doors with their timid gargoyle guards. We never smoked leaning against the cathedral walls like other, braver people did. We were afraid of collapse.

That summer the government instated rolling blackouts of eight-hour periods in order to save energy. My father, who couldn't stop explaining things that we didn't fully understand, had told us that of the country's three power plants only one worked, and not very often, and badly. The other two needed funding, and the nation wasn't going to get a cent because it owed too much to foreign creditors. So, they were not going to work. "Are we going to have to live without electricity forever?" I asked one day, in tears. What did *foreign debt* even mean? Those were the ugliest and saddest words I could imagine. There were no cinemas. There was no music. We weren't allowed to walk down certain streets that were too dark. Sometimes the electricity didn't come back on after the eight hours as promised, and we spent twenty-four hours in the dark. Soccer games were played during the day. There were no batteries or rental generators in the whole city. There were only four hours of TV, eight to midnight, and they didn't show good movies anymore. I didn't want to live like that. Prices went up, too. If I bought cigarettes for my mother in the morning, they cost two pesos; in the afternoon, the same pack would cost three. The names for our apocalypse were energy crisis, hyperinflation, carry trade, due obedience, pink plague. It was 1989 and there was no future.

When a fifteen-year-old girl has no future, she lies in the sun with her whole body coated in Coca-Cola, and her sticky skin draws flies. Or else she falls in love with death and dyes her hair and jeans black. If she can, she buys a lace veil and gloves. Some of my classmates spent their afternoons tanning for an impossible beach. Virginia and I only used the pool to cool off when the heat got to be junglelike. We preferred black clothes and pale skin. We always came home late. If our parents reprimanded us, they did it halfheartedly. I don't really remember any parents being around that summer, except for my dad with all his explanations of the inexplicable. The others were either looking for work or depressed in bed or drinking wine in front of the dark TV or in some consulate office trying to apply for European citizenship so they could escape—any European citizenship would do, but if it was Italian or Spanish, even better.

Virginia and I got obsessed with serial killers that summer. We'd bought a book at the flea market that was held on Sundays in the plaza outside the cathedral. It was in with a pile of junk: Rubik's cubes, very used decks of cards, copper curios, bronze door knockers surely stolen off of old doors, colored bottles, plastic bracelets, old lady necklaces. Some of the objects were for sale, but others could be traded: no one knew exactly what money was worth, so bartering became more reasonable.

The serial killer book was cheap and very tattered. It dedicated a chapter to each of the most famous murderers. We paged through it first with curiosity and then with delight. The only photos were of them, the killers, but the text explained their crimes in detail, including belts made of skin and decorated with nipples and sex with dead girls in dark forests. We traded it for two Limoges porcelain plates from my grandmother's incomplete collection. We read in the cool of the building's stairwell.

I brought up the subject at dinner that night, by the light of candles, over mashed potatoes and an overcooked piece of meat. "Argentina has no serial killers," said my dad as he poured himself some wine. "Unless you count the generals," added my mother; they seemed to be itching for a fight, again. I took a candle to my bed and started reading: we had decided that for now I would keep the book with me, because my parents were more "permissive." Virginia called and asked to come by. It was late, but the lack of electricity had made schedules crazy. It was impossible to sleep with that heat, and in spite of the darkness, people were outside in the street more than ever, fanning themselves, silent in their plastic chairs, waiting for the red moon to explode in the sky or for the stars to give off beams of light that would return our electricity or else put an end to us. The dead electric fans seemed to laugh at the torpor and the occasional muffled sob that broke the silence. That night we read until the candles burned down, and Virginia had to feel her way along the walls back to her apartment.

During the day we'd wander around with the book under an arm. When we told people what it was about, our neighbors and parents and other girls called us morbid. We were sick of people telling us "Argentina has no serial killers." There must be one, we insisted. Didn't they remember Carlitos, "The Angel of Death," a beautiful, evil teenager back in the '70s who had murdered night watchmen and guards when he was committing his robberies? They remembered, vaguely. The heat dulled people, like death. More than Carlitos and his golden curls, people talked to us about a monster of a man, a child killer from the '30s, a second-generation Italian immigrant who'd had giant ears and slept with bird cadavers under his bed and had died in jail in Ushuaia. (My dad wanted to move to Ushuaia: he said there was work down at the end of the world.) But the '30s were so long ago! Not a different time, more like a different planet. Not a single one now? Not one contemporary killer? None. There were cruel criminals, but they murdered their wives, their families, for revenge, for money, out of jealousy—because they were sexist pigs, as my mother said. They didn't kill methodically or for the pure pleasure of it or out of necessity or anxiety or compulsion. When we insinuated that the dictators could be considered serial killers, people got really mad at us: "That's disrespectful."

"My mom said it first," I replied.

"She must have said that without thinking," they'd retort. Others went quiet, thinking that at least there had been no blackouts during the dictatorship.

Virginia and I, admittedly, talked about nothing else. Everything seemed horrible and hard to believe, like the rituals of a different species. The reading lamps that Ed Gein made out of human leather after skinning his victims; the cadavers John Wayne Gacy buried in the crawl space under his house, and his clown makeup when he performed at children's parties; Ted Bundy and his long-haired girls, all of them pretty, all so similar, a doll collection destroyed and abandoned in the mountains. Richard Ramirez, who would sneak into houses at night, silent as a shadow and beautiful as a tornado. "I wish he'd kill me," I said to Virginia once while we looked at his photo: his slanted eyes, rockstar hips, steely cheekbones. At night, in bed, my head on the pillow, I'd put my own hands around my neck and imagine they were Richard's, that he was squeezing until all my air was gone, until he broke my vertebrae. I knew that he had raped the women, too, but that never appeared in my nighttime fantasies, which were delicate and virginal.

My parents did get fed up once and threatened to throw the book into the trash. Wasn't there enough death as it was? they asked, referring to the dictatorship and torturers; they didn't understand that Virginia and I were into a different sort of hell, an unreal, noisy inferno of masks and chainsaws, of pentagrams painted on the wall in blood and heads stored in the freezer.

Our routine was simple. During the day we tried to get cool in the shade, and if that didn't work, we swam in the pool; we never sunbathed. At dusk we sat on the sidewalk or in the plaza, and if by some miracle one of us had gotten our hands on batteries, we'd listen to music on the tape deck. I missed music more than anything; my meticulously labeled cassettes were dead in their drawer because even if the electricity came back at night I could listen for only a few hours—people in the house had to sleep, and my headphones were broken and I couldn't buy new ones. If neither of us had batteries, which was more often the case, we read our serial killer book out loud in the plaza in front of the unstable cathedral, smoking cigarettes stolen from fathers and mothers and uncles and aunts.

We also smoked in the stairwell of our building, which was always cool. No one ever tried to tell us we couldn't smoke tobacco. You couldn't see a thing in the stairwell, but at least it wasn't hot in there, since it was untouched by the sun: another building blocked the light, and plus, the stairwell didn't have windows. The cigarette tips lit up in the dark with every drag, orange like fireflies, and whenever anyone came down the stairs, sometimes with a flashlight, other times feeling their way along the walls, they ignored us. Everyone ignored us. If someone asked about the sharp and still unfamiliar (to adults) smell of weed, we told them it was incense and they believed us. They bought incense, too, from the hippies in the plaza selling useless objects—people would often burn it as an offering to some plaster saint, Saint Cajetan or the Virgin, when they prayed for work.

It was boring, that apocalyptic summer, and it seemed like it would never end. But all that changed when our neighbor on the seventh floor, whom we knew only as Carrasco, killed his wife and daughter. He did it at night and we found out the next day: there were police and firemen everywhere. He fled in the early morning, and the few hours of TV transmission began airing the police sketch of his face constantly; there was even a reward being offered.

*

Here, I need to add a quick parenthetical note. It had been two years since my parents and I had moved to that neighborhood called Las Torres. The buildings there were not projects: those kinds of well-intentioned developments didn't exist in our country anymore. They were just cheap housing. Buildings of more than fifteen floors with very thin walls that let all kinds of sounds through: shouts, moans of pleasure, fights, crying babies, musical instruments. All the apartments were the same: a living/dining room, a small kitchen where the front door was, and a large bedroom, which most people divided in two using a wardrobe or screen. There was an unintended consequence to having the kitchens so close to the front doors: the hallways always smelled of food, which was fine if someone was cooking a delicious tomato sauce or some seasoned delicacy, but it was awful, nauseating, when the smell floating in the air was from fried food, fish, boiled cauliflower, even grilled meat, which smells delicious at first but starts to have a whiff of rot once it stagnates.

Virginia lived on the seventh floor, same as the murderer and his family. She didn't share the only bedroom with her parents, but instead slept in the living room. That seemed better to me: she had some privacy. When I suggested the idea to my dad, he seemed hurt, maybe offended. He asked if I thought our apartment wasn't good enough, and he apologized for being unemployed and poor. I just repeated the truth: I preferred the living room because that was where the TV was, and, if there was electricity, I could watch it; also, I could read until late without bothering them, or listen to the radio on low. He didn't seem convinced. He mumbled something about this dissolute life and how I've had it with this country, we'll get out of here if we can, honey. Whenever he talked about leaving, it meant there was a speech coming about what a mistake my Spanish grandfather had made when he'd taken Argentine citizenship. When he did that, he had robbed me, his granddaughter, of the possibility of inheriting the longed-for passport, because the Spanish state only recognized the nationality of first-generation children. I didn't care. I didn't want to go to Spain. I wanted to sleep in the living room and I wanted to listen to music again.

My father talked about the future, but I didn't understand. It was as far away as the '30s and the child killer who had died in Ushuaia. My dad worried too much, same as Virginia's mom, who went around in a nightgown wondering out loud what the kids were going to do, what she and her family were going to do, what was going to happen. I was embarrassed for Virginia's mom; Virginia was too. Once, we found her all worked up in the stairwell with tears dried on her cheeks; she was fat and it was hard for her to carry the shopping bags up the seven flights of stairs to her apartment. We helped her without a word. Of course, the building had an elevator, but what if the electricity went out and someone got stuck inside? It happened a lot in other buildings, supposedly, and sometimes it took the firemen hours to come. Occasionally we organized as a group to carry bags up, and the youngest of us competed to see who could run up the most floors without stopping. I could only do five: I had to stop, my back soaked in sweat, tongue hanging out and heart knocking at my ribs. Virginia, who played volleyball, made it to the seventh floor with no problem.

Beside the apartment buildings was a small and badly stocked shopping center. The butcher and fish shop—one store—only had hake; some really small, malnourished chickens; and beef that was hard and stringy and only useful for milanesas or stew. The vegetable shop was better, but the fruit was expensive. The kiosk was the only place we liked because Pity, the owner, always put chocolates on sale, bought flowers to brighten up the kiosk, and had Rolito, a brand of dry ice in bags that kept the beer cold. We all loved Pity, even more so since one old and pathetic neighbor had insulted him for being a fag. "Better a fag than a collaborator," Pity had retorted, and that time my dad hadn't wanted to explain what they were talking about, but I think I understood.

That cheap apartment complex had a swimming pool, as I've said, and there we floated in perpetual battle against the heat. The only problem was that, according to even the most basic safety rules, the pool should have had a lifeguard on duty, even though it wasn't very deep. And also someone to clean it so it didn't stagnate. The neighbors couldn't pay an employee, so they did the job themselves, but they did it badly. The water had a certain stink to it, its surface murky, dead bugs floating in the corners. There was always someone watching out for the littlest kids and asking people to please not run around the pool because if they fell into the water they could drown or hit their heads on the edge. I doubt that those spontaneous custodians could even swim themselves. My dad took care of the pool for a while, and he doesn't know how to swim.

Carrasco, the murderer, regularly went to the pool. He swam with the long strokes of a professional and emerged shaking himself dry like a dog. He didn't talk much, but he seemed nice enough. No one knew what he did for a living, but not many men were working that year. His wife and daughter didn't come to the pool, and he never explained why. We figured they, like us, weren't fans of the sun, or else it was bad for them, because they were both really pale, especially the wife. Even paler than Virginia and me, and we did our best to be creatures of the night, with our lace gloves and dark glasses. Virginia said that no sounds of fighting ever came from their apartment on the seventh floor. Just music because the wife was or had been a dancer. Anyway, they were a small and silent family; not even their kitchen smells betrayed them. They must have cooked a lot of rice and pasta, foods that didn't smell and seep out into the hallway air.

*

The crime did us all good. The four hours of nightly TV were dedicated entirely to Carrasco and his murdered family. When the transmission ended, the expectation and anticipation of finding out more details of the case the next day helped us get through the night. Helped us forget, for example, that Pity, the kiosk owner we all loved, was back in the hospital. The ambulance had come, this time without the siren, and people were saying he wouldn't be going home this time. We thought his family wanted him to die, because the kiosk was getting fewer and fewer customers: after the fight with the old man, everyone knew he had AIDS. "Sure, we appreciate him, but we don't want to get sick; it's just awful how he touches everything he sells," we heard one woman say, and Virginia wanted to spit on her. That woman wasn't alone: a lot of neighbors were afraid they would catch AIDS if they bought candy from him. Not us. We had learned in school how the virus spread, and we knew it didn't stick to chocolates or bags of potato chips. We tried to explain, but it was no use.

We hated ignorant people, and if we could get our hands

on any money we would go to the kiosk and buy cookies and soft drinks and powdered juice—anything processed or artificial. We liked everything fake: Fizz candies that bubbled on the tongue, Blue Moon ice cream that was a sky-blue color, anything that would dissolve or expand in water. We also liked Pity and didn't want him to die. He was thin and beautiful, with long fingers covered with rings and eyes that were a little yellow, like a cat's. I talked to him about serial killers one day and he added Thierry Paulin to the list, a Frenchman who'd killed only elderly people in Paris. "Your book only has murderers from the US, I think," he said.

"My mom says serial killers only exist in the US," I told him.

"I don't think that's true," he said. "I'm sure they just sell them better there."

Carrasco had killed his dancer wife in the early morning, while she slept. Stabbed her through the sheet (that detail disturbed me—what was she doing under a sheet in heat like that?). The investigators knew because he'd left her covered, and the holes in the sheet coincided with all the stab wounds in the body, except for the ones on the neck and cheek. He had used a special knife, the kind used for cutting bones at a barbecue. Carrasco's wife was shy and quiet but spectacularly beautiful, like a model. She hid it, made herself uglier on purpose, but it was impossible not to notice her when she went up and down the stairs on her strong legs, with her trained muscles and long arms. Even though she wore her hair pulled up, when she went by it smelled like winter flowers, and she had thin lips but very white teeth. I was disappointed when I found out that she was a traditional folk dancer. I'd pictured her as a classical ballerina, and I imagined her on pointe, with theatrical makeup and a bun, as the black swan.

Anyway, no one was all that worried about the fate of the poor dancer wife, considering what Carrasco had done to their daughter. The girl was younger than us and was always at school: she went to both sessions and came home at six in the evening, when it was almost dark out. She wore a strange uniform: in those days, most private schools required the standard gray jumper, white shirt, and blue tie or bow. Carrasco's daughter wore a plaid jumper and a light-pink shirt. What school did she go to? Some cheap Catholic school. Virginia and I attended public schools and knew nothing about God or nuns; we had never learned to pray. After Carrasco killed his wife and daughter, we asked a Catholic neighbor lady to teach us the Our Father. We prayed in the stairwell. I cried because I thought our obsession with murderers had summoned death, even though Carrasco wasn't a serial killer. I cried above all for the girl and her green jumper, which was too big for her, surely because they'd wanted to save money by getting one that would last her a few years, one she could grow into.

I didn't see her hanging from the window. Over time, so many people would swear they'd seen her dangling there, inert, her face toward the building and her legs separated in the air, that it became a joke, that lying "I was there." It's true that Pity's brother had seen—he had insomnia while Pity was in his death throes, and he went out to the balcony to smoke. He lived in the building across from ours, right above the kiosk. He looked up and there was the girl, a sheet tied around her neck, hanging from the window. That night there was some wind, and he said that her face hit against the building and made a muffled, fleshy sound, the sound of her nose being smashed with every gust of hot air. He called the police. How had the knot her father tied borne the girl's weight? Why didn't it come undone, why didn't the sheet break? After all, she was ten years old and she wasn't small: she was tall and a little chubby; no one could explain how that sheet held up or why the heavy body hadn't fallen. The police used a ladder to get her down and more people saw that part, but still not so many, because the best view was blocked by the fire truck's tall ladder. The police wouldn't let the cameras record them unhooking the sheet, and there are no images of her battered face. There was more consideration back in 1989, or maybe the detail of the little girl tossed about by the wind was too much, even for programs that were eager for ratings.

The girl was already dead when her father hung her. He had stabbed her several times with a different knife than he'd used on her mother—a small kitchen knife, common and domestic—and let her bleed out on the dining room floor. Then he tied her to the bars of the bedroom window as if she were a flag or a doll. He tied her in a complicated way, looping the sheet under her armpits and around her neck. She was hanging like that in the night for a little over an hour. If it hadn't been for Pity's brother's anxiety and his cigarette, dawn would have broken on her dead and hanging, her chocolate-colored hair burning under the sun.

My family and I didn't hear a thing from our apartment on the sixth floor. The people in 6B, right under the Carrascos' place, were on vacation: they had a house on the coast that they were going to sell in less than six months. Later, when the neighbors had to made statements before the judge, some of them mentioned having heard screams, but they said, ashamed, that they hadn't thought about getting involved. Carrasco and the dancer were always quiet, and they'd thought it must be a rare but harmless spat. Carrasco was a jealous man; we knew that much. That day, the dancer had gotten home a little late after picking her daughter up from school. There had been a transportation strike and everyone had had trouble getting home, but Carrasco, people thought, hadn't found that argument convincing. No one had heard him say that, but the investigators supposed the fight had been along those lines because the dancer had told the vegetable vendor, "My husband doesn't like it when I get home after sunset, but the city was impossible today." Carrasco didn't kill her during the fight, in any case. The neighbors weren't wrong about that. He did it later, while his wife and daughter were asleep. If there were screams, they were few and short-lived.

On TV they suggested that the dancer—her name was Luisina—had a lover and was planning to run away with him.

"You think it's true?" Virginia asked.

I doubt it, I thought. Where could they even have gone? Unless he was rich. She didn't have the money to leave Argentina: if they were neighbors of ours, it meant they were pretty poor. And moving within the country—what was the point? It was the same everywhere: no electricity, no money, no work, no spirit.

"She could have been like those women who have kids during a war," said Virginia as she peered critically at her legs, bared by her short shorts: she couldn't find a good hair removal cream because her favorite one was French and imports had stopped.

"What women?"

"I saw a movie about it once. There are some women who like to get pregnant when there's a war. They say that giving life is like combating death. Some shit like that. It's a mindset."

"But if she had a boyfriend, where would they have run away to? You can't even get gas."

"Yeah. Why can't they import gas, anyway, do you know?"

"Same reason as everything else: because we don't have the money to pay for it. My dad says the military is going to over-throw the government."

Virginia yanked a hair out of her leg with her mom's rusty tweezers.

"Damn, it hurts to do it this way," she said.

"So use wax."

"I don't know how. It burns."

We found out from the newspapers that the girl's name was Clara ("Clarita"). We thought about her there, dangling alone out the window at night; we thought about the sound of her body falling, if it had fallen. My mother started to smoke even more and to dream about the girl. But the immediate effect was that we were no longer allowed to go out alone because they were afraid Carrasco would come back. We had to explain things to our parents laboriously, knowledgeably. Yes, true, murderers often return to the scene of the crime, so we could expect Carrasco to turn up some night, though he was unlikely to take such a risk with the police watching the building. If he came back, he might stop at the corner, for example: it's not that murderers had to retrace their exact steps. They just wanted to look, sometimes from a distance.

David Berkowitz, the Son of Sam, who committed his murders in New York in the '70s, also during a period of power outages, went back because looking at the scenes of his crimes brought him pleasure—for him it was like looking at naked girls. We thought it was our duty to explain what we had learned because we felt guilty. Carrasco didn't leave a note? When they are insatiable, killers leave something written. The Lipstick Killer had written on a wall: "For heavens sake catch me before I kill more I cannot control myself."

"I don't think Carrasco is like that," Virginia said. "He only wanted to kill his wife and daughter, who knows why." The insinuations about Luisina's lover always annoyed my mom—it was like they were blaming her, she said. Did he just *have* to kill her because she was going to leave him—are we all crazy? And what did the little girl have to do with it? "Well, he must have thought of the girl as a cheater's daughter," said my father from the sofa, and my mother, horrified, yelled at him: "There it is, just look at how these manly men can interpret and justify each other."

"I'm not justifying anything, what are you talking about?" retorted my father, and I grabbed Virginia by the hand and pulled her out of the apartment so she wouldn't have to witness another ridiculous fight. "My parents hardly ever fight," she told me once we were sitting on the steps and lighting joints of Paraguayan weed that reeked of chemicals. "They're like ghosts."

That night I couldn't fall asleep right away; my dad's snoring kept me awake. And though I felt like I was going crazy, I thought about Richard Ramirez. About his almond-shaped eyes and his dark hair and brown skin, his thin body and his gapped-tooth smile. But when I closed my eyes, Richard slowly transformed into Carrasco: I almost smelled the chlorine on his damp skin after swimming, felt the wetness of his hair that he also wore a little long, and heard the knife blade scrape the bed frame. I got up and ran to lock myself in the bathroom, but I couldn't throw up. Maybe we had it wrong in spite of all our studies of murderer behavior; maybe our parents were right and Carrasco could come back, sneak into my room, slit my throat with that blade that smelled of barbecue, of charcoal and burnt meat.

*

Our parents were right about one thing: Carrasco did come back. To this day, Virginia and I argue about whether it was a hallucination, all in our heads. But I think it was him, and when I tell the story I always see Carrasco in the shadows, smell his scent of aftershave, sweat, and hungry breath, the same one people have on the train in the early morning when they go to work without having eaten breakfast, on empty stomachs. The stairs between the sixth and seventh floors were completely dark even during the day and without power outages because they didn't have windows. It was a cheap construction; not only was it ugly, it also made you feel closed in, it inspired claustrophobia, the urge to flee and the certainty of being unable to escape. The landing where we went to stay cool in the afternoons and smoke in peace was the darkest of them all. Without the light from the hallways, without the elevator's light, it was like being in a tomb that was spacious and bustling, since the neighbors came and went, always talking about the fates of Carrasco, Luisina, and Clarita.

We were in the stairwell when we found out about Pity's death and about what had happened after: none of the funeral parlors would accept his body, and his wake was being held in his apartment, by candlelight no less. We decided to go over there right away: we just had to cross the street. His brother hugged us in the doorway and said, "Thank you so much for coming, but there's no need for you to come in; you're very young and it could be a shock." We told him we wanted to say goodbye to Pity because he had been good to us: he'd recorded tapes for us, let us make photocopies for free when we didn't have money, and he'd gotten Virginia an incredible nail polish that made her hands sparkle when she moved them, as if they were radiating fairy dust.

There weren't many people in the room. Pity's parents were in one dark corner, hugging, and there were three or four other very serious adults who must have been relatives. Then there were several young men, surely friends of his, who were very thin, very well dressed, and crying. On the bed, the shadows sharpened Pity's face, and he looked like a little old woman wrapped in a white sheet. Pity, who had been so handsome with his long hair and perfect teeth. We didn't stay long: Virginia said that with the heat the body would start to stink any minute, and we slipped away without saying goodbye. We weren't tired, as Pity's face and his thin body under the sheets had made us nervous, so we went back to the dark stairwell. Only the lighter's flare illuminated our faces; we used it often because the weed was damp. "They piss on it to preserve it," Virginia said, but I didn't want to believe that the acidic aftertaste that made us cough was the urine of the dealer or whoever it was who had packed the marijuana bricks away on the Paraguayan border.

That night, in addition to the pot, we were smoking Marlboros: a real score, because it was a very expensive brand. Virginia had stolen half a pack from her uncle. In order to relax, we decided not to talk about Pity or Carrasco or the girls Ted Bundy murdered (Virginia liked Ted Bundy, but she never told me whether she had fantasies like mine with Richard. She was always into guys like Bundy, conventionally attractive and secretly violent). We talked about how to spray-paint T-shirts and get stencils to make letters because we wanted to write phrases on them, though we were still debating which ones. We also discussed whether it was a good idea to use crepe paper to dye our hair, or if we should keep on with the cheap henna from the perfume store. "It's going to make us go bald," said Virginia, "our hair is falling out," and she clicked the lighter on again.

Then we heard footsteps on the stairs, and the person who was coming down stopped in front of us because we were blocking the way. We couldn't make out the shape very well. It was a black splotch, human but unfamiliar. It looked at us; though we couldn't see its eyes, we could distinguish the damp shine of its gaze. It was a man. Virginia said hi, sure that it was a neighbor on his way downstairs to get some air or see if the pizzeria was still open, but when he didn't answer or move, our stomachs filled with a cold fear, and I knew it was Carrasco and he was going to hang us out a window the way people hung Argentine flags during the World Cup. He was going to hang us by our necks and let us swing there until the cheap cement destroyed our faces like it had his daughter's. I don't know how

I did it, but I stood up and took off running and Virginia followed me, screaming. We ran down the stairs in the darkness, stumbling, and the next day our legs were covered in bruises and we even had scrapes on our cheeks. It was like running through a maze even though we knew the way out, and I swear I felt Carrasco's breath with its hungry stench at my back, and I heard him panting the way a smoker or an exhausted man gasps for air.

When we got to the ground floor, the policeman who had been guarding the building's entrance stopped us and we stammered out the story of what we'd seen, and we shouted and insulted him too, telling him he was worthless, that he had let the murderer in, how had he not realized? The cop told us to be quiet and called a squad car. They gave the order to evacuate. Because of us, all the neighbors ended up in the street, in the welcoming heat of the night, asking what we had seen, and we talked about Carrasco and his silence, his unmistakable smell of men's cologne and sweat. Some women decided to leave that night to go to their mothers' or other relatives' houses; others, fewer, said they would spend the night at a rooming house with their families. The men seemed incapable of deciding whether to stay or go. We realized, too, that there weren't many single people in our building. My mother dried my tears and hugged me too tightly, so tightly that I had to squirm away so she'd leave me alone, and she looked at me with sadness and the disappointment of rejection. Virginia's parents were much less expressive, which I preferred.

The police searched all the apartments and the hallways and stairwells and didn't find anything or anybody. One of the cops led us to the squad car and tried to scare us by saying we shouldn't make things up because that was perjury and perjury was a crime. He also treated us with contempt and looked at our tits a little: we were both wearing tight black tank tops. He gave us some bullshit about the boy who cried wolf and I thought, You're the only wolf here, I bet you're a torturer—back then, there were no cops from the dictatorship in prison yet. You're worse than Carrasco, I thought, and I wanted to spit on him, but I held back because I knew what cops were capable of. And also because right when I was thinking about spitting on him the electricity came back on, and the neighbors sighed in relief because there was light and the cops declared that the building was completely safe. Doubtless they also told the neighbors that Virginia and I were lying. But no one got mad: "They're spooked, poor things," I heard people say. "And with good reason."

The sun came out: no one had slept hardly at all that night, and we watched as workers carried Pity's body out from the building across from us; they wore gloves and masks as if they were transporting something toxic. My parents made breakfast and then went to bed. I locked the apartment door and sat down alone in the kitchen. We have to move, I thought. We can't go on living in this building where the murderer is hiding and where I'm sure the murdered dancer is going to appear any time now, dancing down the dark stairwells. We can't go on living close to the wall where Clarita hung for an hour, Clarita swaying in the wind like a piñata; soon, as well, we would start to hear the pounding of her face in our dreams, the wet pounding of her face against her own blood and the remains of her nose and chin and lips, blood and flesh that decorated our building and that the firemen hadn't been able to wash off entirely, nor the rain, because we all know that bloodstains are the hardest things to clean, even once they're impossible to see.

SOROCHE

MÓNICA OJEDA

TRANSLATED BY SARAH BOOKER AND NOELLE DE LA PAZ

LO LLAMAN MAL DE AIRE, MAL DE ALTURA, MAL DE
MONTAÑA, MAL DE PÁRAMO, APUNAMIENTO, SOROCHE...

VIVIANA

THEY CALL IT AIR SICKNESS, ALTITUDE SICKNESS, MOUNTAIN sickness, sick from the highlands, sick from the plateaus, sick with soroche, but whenever you get it they want you to chew coca leaves like a damn alpaca, and that's what I don't like. I find it disgusting. I was once given coca tea, and it was the most repulsive thing I'd ever tasted in my life. I know what it's like to be way up high, you know? I've been to La Paz, to Quito, to Cuzco. I've traveled a lot because I like getting to know new places and new cultures. I travel at least twice a year, and not to just any old continent, but to countries where the landscape is harsh. I don't do chic tourism, no sir. I dive headfirst into adventure, and sometimes there are consequences. Anyway, I assume you've heard what it feels like when soroche gets you good, but I'll explain it to you anyway because I want you to understand there's nothing I could have done. I was barely able to stay standing, and at times not even that. Look, it feels like there's a ghost inside you, like you're filled with a heavy, malignant air that makes it hard to breathe. At first you don't notice: you just feel tired and your heart races—you know?—like you're running a marathon. You can handle that; it's not so bad. But then it gets ugly: you get dizzy, your head hurts, you vomit, you tremble. Ay, it's the ugliest thing! Your field of vision shrinks, becomes a tunnel the light can't penetrate. So how was I going to do anything? As we climbed the mountain, I felt the ghost made of air grabbing me by my bones and dragging me down to the ends of the earth. If you know what it's like to have soroche, you'll understand. I couldn't have done anything under those circumstances. Nothing at all.

KARINA

We took the long, difficult trail. We wanted to get the full experience. No thank you, but do you have sparkling water? If you could serve it with a slice of lemon, even better. Thank you, dear. I was saying we chose the longer route with the full understanding we could return before sunset. That was the plan. And I remember perfectly that's how we decided on it, because I told the girls I had to send an email to my agent, something about a contract I'm getting ready to sign with an important publisher. Thank you, thank you, but did you read my last book? How flattering! Yes, it's dedicated to Renato, my late husband. He is and always will be the love of my life. Excuse me. Don't worry, I have a tissue. I hope you aren't bothered by how affectionate I am: I call everyone dear. Let me know if it bothers you, dear. We were happily climbing the mountain and chatting. It had been quite some time since we'd traveled, not to mention that kind of destination. If I'm being honest, hippie tourism isn't really my thing, but I wanted to spend time with my friends far away from responsibilities, work, children, boyfriends, husbands, gossip... Well, you get it. We also planned it with Ana in mind, of course. The poor thing was in terrible shape, and she had good reason to be depressed. We all tried to cheer her up, distract her, but that doesn't mean she didn't have good reason. The trip was my idea. I'm the one with the good ideas, ha! I didn't pick the destination, though, because if it had been up to me, we would've gone to a more modern city, maybe in Europe or the United States, the kind with bookstores featured in rom-coms and famous malls. I'm a writer who enjoys big cities, cultural activities, and fashion. I'm quite stylish, as you can tell. I'm elegant like Chimamanda Ngozi Adichie, don't you think? Black women these days are so beautiful! Anyway, I gave Ana a book by Chimamanda, a feminist one so she'd quickly get over the thing with her husband...excuse me, ex-husband, but I doubt she read it. She isn't a good reader. Not the brightest bulb, the poor thing. That's why the husband did what he did to her: because he could. No one would've ever done that to me.

NICOLE

We've always been best friends. We met in high school, which is where people make their true friends, the lifelong ones. Our high school was and is one of the most respected, where the children of well-off, hardworking, God-fearing people who want to thrive go. After all, people stick with those who have the same values. Furthermore, our families have always been close. For example, Vivi and Kari's mothers used to play tennis at the same club, and my dad and Anita's dad were lawyers at the same firm. Now we all live practically on top of one another, and our children are close friends. Carlitos and Juanito fought over a girl, but it isn't a big deal; boys will be boys. The point is, we're inseparable: we go to the same church, we organize neighborhood meetings, we take Zumba classes at the local gym. Like sisters. That's not to say we don't have our differences. We had and still have them, but we know how to get over them. If maturity has given us anything it's the perspective and patience to understand a person's defects, to accept that if we want God to forgive our wrongdoings, we must also forgive those who wrong us. It isn't like they've wronged me; it's just a saying. In reality we almost never argue about important things, only stupid ones. Total nonsense. We all get annoyed every now and then with those closest to us; it's normal. For example, the way Kari takes the lead even though no one needs or asks her to sometimes bothers me. She has a—how shall I put it?—dictatorial personality. She thinks she's superior because she's written a book on Catholic feminism that, by the way, brings up confusing questions like what to do about lesbians. She's a very intelligent woman, no one's taking that away from her, but there are greater virtues like consistency and humility, things she doesn't put into practice. Vivi's also arrogant, though for other reasons. She's obsessed with fitness and has a way of telling people they look bad without really saying it, just giving them a look. I think it's awful that she goes around judging other people's physiques so harshly, especially when she herself wouldn't look so good if it weren't for her husband's money. It's a secret, she'd kill me if she found out I'm spreading this, but she's had more than five surgeries, and not exactly for health reasons. I recognize they've made her look magnificent, but as a girl she was completely flat front and back. No joke, she looked like a boy. My point is, when it comes to someone you love, it's normal to want to kill them one day and not the next. I've gotten so mad I've spit in Karina's face. Can you imagine? The woman who looks at everyone else as if she were above them. Yes, a big glob in the middle of her enormous writer nose. And Vivi? I once fantasized about popping her implants. Don't get me wrong, I adore both of them, but God clearly still has lessons to teach them. For example, what happened to Anita was nothing but a divine test. Her sin has always been pride: She felt like she was the best wife, the best mother, the best friend, the best Christian. She was also the only one in the group who'd never had her heart broken. It's not like her suffering makes me happy, but maybe she needed that dose of humility, that painful experience that's left the rest of us feeling renewed and stronger. Tragedy is good for some people. For example, I love Anita more now, after what her ex did to her. I feel compassion for her; I feel sorry for her. Even with what happened on the mountain. Yes, I believe it now. Pain unites people, and we're closer than ever.

ANA

I had soroche too, but that's not what made me jump. You know what I'm talking about because you've seen the video;

don't play dumb. I see it in your face, young man, in the way you look at me: with disgust, with embarrassment. You haven't stopped staring at my chest since you got here. Do you think I don't know what my breasts look like? I've probably watched the video more times than you or anyone else. Over and over, crying, screaming, pulling my hair out. I know quite well what I look like. I know what everybody who watched it thinks: that I'm a fat, disgusting old hag. That's what they think: that I'm a cow with grotesque, saggy teats. A repulsive, mooing cow. Mooo.

VIVIANA

You'd have to be a complete dick to do something like that to Anita. A real pig. I watched the video and thought, poor Anita! The truth is the truth, and the truth is she looks awfully fat, like a walrus, oof! Hideous, the poor girl. Don't go believing she was depressed over the divorce: it wasn't that, it was because everyone got to see her jiggly, saggy, deflated tits, her gargantuan nipples, her cellulitis, her varicose veins, the horrific way her blubber moved while—well you know, right?—as if making waves. It's kind of amusing, but only a little. I remember details so disgusting it's better I don't tell you. Anyway, that's what she found so hard to bear. That, and only that, is what put her into a depression. We all felt bad about it, so we planned the trip. We wanted her to change her mindset, to see the bright side. In spite of everything, I understand Anita, you know? If people had seen me like that, I'd die. It's different, of course, since I'm in shape, but I imagine what happened to her and it makes my hair stand on end. I know Anita, and I know she couldn't stop thinking about the video. Poor thing didn't want to leave the house or even be with her children. I told her, "Anita, it's no big deal, we'll go to the gym a few more times a week if you want, I'll be your trainer and I'll make you a babe," but she never got back to me. That's one of her biggest flaws: laziness. I've spent years telling her she needs an exercise routine specifically for weight loss and muscle toning, for her own good, you know? If she'd listened to me, at least she would've looked different in the video. At least she would've looked good, which is what matters.

KARINA

It's true Ana wasn't talking much, that she cried at night and looked somewhat lost during the day, that she didn't eat or laugh at our jokes, that she locked herself in the bathroom for long stretches of time. But, dear, we didn't know she was having such a hard time. How would we? We aren't in her head, and we aren't psychologists. It certainly was a delicate moment for her; that's why we told her people would forget about the video even if it wasn't true. People in our circle don't forget that kind of thing. Ana will be able to return to her normal life, of course, and no one will stop talking to her or anything. She'll still be the vice president of the neighborhood association and the director of the church choir. She'll still be invited to parties and meetings. No one will take away her position or social status. What I mean is that, at least in appearance, everything will go on as before. The problem, dear, is that Ana knows, and we know, that no one will ever look at her the same way. No one will respect her or believe in the image she's sold us of herself. It's too late, we've seen the truth. From now on people will pity her most of the time, and that's terrible for a woman. I feel sorry for her. I suggested we take a trip together because I feel so bad for her, or as Nicole says, out of commiseration. Ana was definitely on board from the beginning. Anyway, we checked into a nice hotel, took a walk around the historical center, and ate dinner at one of the city's traditional restaurants. The altitude tired us out quickly, but it wasn't anything out of this world. We woke up early the next morning because that's what Viviana's plan dictated. She decided the views were worth climbing a ways up the mountain. "Let's go hiking!" she said. If they'd asked me, I would've chosen a tall building with an elevator, ha! Exploring in high heels is very in. Viviana always boasts about being in shape. It's part of her personality. I don't know what she'll do when she realizes she's no longer a pretty little thing and that we've all noticed the work she's had done. Anyway, we climbed the mountain chatting about random things, about the Zumba instructor, decor, our kids, upcoming parties, and above all, avoiding any mention of the video, but it was there, just like the soroche. As I said before, we all felt a little off because of the altitude, but we were fine. Dear, I know Viviana says she felt like she was going to die, but that isn't true. She was happy with the excursion. It was later, on the mountain, when we all got sick. We followed the trail and enjoyed the landscape, which was lovely, just like the one I describe in my book. And I'd never been on a mountain, but I have a good imagination. I confess I've considered writing about what happened to Ana. A novel, perhaps, with a character inspired by her... I think I'd know how to transmit her anguish and her misgivings because, and anyone who knows me will tell you this, I'm tremendously empathetic. It's one of my distinguishing features. Anyway, while we were climbing, we realized we were up pretty high, and that's when someone, I think it was Nicole, said she was feeling strange. It's possible

Viviana was also feeling sick, but given that she likes to brag about her resilience and physical fitness, she didn't tell us. I, on the other hand, said my head was heavy and my arms felt like liquid. We kept walking anyway, I don't know why. I suppose it was for Ana and because we'd already spent an hour climbing uphill. I'm sure she also had soroche, which made her see what she saw. It isn't like Ana went crazy, she just lost it for an instant. Things happen. Sadness and lack of oxygen can cloud one's thinking. You can't judge her. It was the altitude. You see, dear? I'm all empathy.

NICOLE

You don't do that to a woman our age. Men post videos of their partners when they're twenty-something, thirty-something. If they do that to you when you're young, it's humiliating, but life goes on. At our age, though, we're already gracefully going downhill. I've always been told, "Never do anything you'd be embarrassed for others to see you doing." Those are wise words. I hope Anita learns from this tough lesson. God knows what He is doing and never gives us more than we can bear. Amen.

ANA

What was I thinking about as we climbed the mountain, kid?
I was thinking about myself on the bed with my legs spread
open. About my fat thighs, wrinkled with peaks and craters
like an orange peel. About my blue, red, and green veins swollen like sea worms. About my fingers making circles on my
clitoris thinking I'm sexy when clearly, obviously, definitively,
I am not. About my purple teats. About my dimwitted bulldog
tongue. About my vagina's huge labia, dark and depraved. About
how he makes me roll over and the camera falls into a corner
and all you can see are my tits like two rotting eggplants. I'm
thinking about my mooing, mooo. About my bovine expression.
About the bushy black fuzz covering my flabby belly. About
the pathetic face I make when I think I'm being sexy. About
the Cesarean scar etched all the way across me like a centi-
pede. About my sumo wrestler body, my elephant body, my
seal body, thrashing around nauseatingly, ridiculously, repul-
sively. About how he picks up the camera and zooms in on my
anus with its hemorrhoids and sticks his finger in, and I bleed
and poop. About his voice when he says to me, "You're a disgusting slut." "Slut, slut, slut, slut, slut." "Your stench is going
to make me vomit all over you." "Filthy whore." "Shit-stained

whore." About how I moo, mooo. About my flat ass. About the ridiculous movements I make when I think I look sexy. About how I am, beyond any doubt, the most vomitous person on the planet. About my friends' faces when they look at me. About my children's faces when they look at me. About my neighbors' and acquaintances' faces when they look at me. About the nausea they all surely feel at the sight of me. About my foul, unsavory, repellent, revolting body believing itself sexy. About the pathetic, sorry sound of my blubber smacking against his hard, athletic body. About the dark brown skin of my inner thighs. About the wart on my back. About how unbearably obese I look, especially from overhead. About my crudely cut pinky nail. About the yellowish corns on my heels. About my hyena wrinkles. About the pathetic, sorry sound of my pubic mound ramming against his abdomen. About my unwaxed armpits. About my armadillo skin, my manatee skin, my turtle skin, my rat skin, my caiman skin, my tapir skin, my cockroach skin. About how he doesn't cum and loses his erection. About how it makes sense he loses his erection. About how it's a miracle he got hard in the first place. About my scaly elbows that in the light of the room look like psoriasis. About how the overhead view not only makes me look unbearably obese, but also reveals the nascent yet inevitable baldness at my crown, pale and shiny like an old knee. About how I have dangling tits of stored blubber on my back. About the hair growing around my nipples. About how I sweat like a pig, and my sweat drips all over the sheets and my African rhinoceros body. About how it makes me gag to see that much sweat and the yellowish tint it leaves on the pillow. About how I'm not just ugly but repugnant, nauseating, hippopotamish. About the bloodstains and shitstains on the duvet that are visible in almost every shot. About the rolls that go all the way up to my neck. About my stinking slobber that drips onto the bed and makes me look like a bulldog more than anything. About how, ever since the video, people are repulsed by the sight of me, even though they hide it to avoid hurting my feelings. About how their act of hiding it to avoid hurting my feelings hurts my feelings. About how I'm surrounded not by love, but by shame. About my enormous double chin that completely engulfs my jawline. About how I'm no longer young or pretty, and no one will desire me ever again because desire is something that's inspired only by beauty and beauty is young and I am no longer young or attractive, but a gorilla, a killer whale, a bison. About how awful it is to be so hideous and yet so alive and to exist in the midst of the most absolute beauty, waiting forever and ever for someone to desire the undesirable, waiting forever and ever for someone to cherish my body and make it beautiful with his love. About the size and color of my hemorrhoids. About my belly button folding in on itself, closed up by my belly fat. About my non-existent waistline. About my sunburnt foot. About the enormous wings of fat under my arms. About how I grip my legs and spread them wide enough to clearly show him shoving his fist into my vagina, letting in air and releasing a queef. About just how long a two-minute-and-thirty-seven-second video can be. About the size and color of my clitoris. About how I will never again kiss or be kissed passionately. About my slobbery tongue, reaching. About the way I ask him to hold me, and he doesn't. About how no one will ever hold me naked again. About how I clench my teeth and fake an orgasm that only I know I didn't have. About how deformed and monstrous my face is when I fake it. About how pathetic I am for having thought, all my life, that I was moaning and not mooing. About the cruelty of time. About how the video ends on the whites of my eyes. About love and ugliness. About how ugliness always wins.

VIVIANA

I didn't catch the moment Ana pulled down her pants. What I did see was the look of bewilderment on Nicole's face, and so I turned around to find Ana in a squat, peeing. Just like that.

Outrageous! You wouldn't know this, but that was something none of us had ever done in front of each other, let alone outdoors, like animals. We were stunned, we couldn't believe it. And after what was in the video…it was surreal. We didn't know how to react or what the hell to do. Someone laughed awkwardly, I think, probably me. We said, "Anita, please," but she didn't even look at us—you know?—like she was in her own universe, entire galaxies away. It was a bizarre moment with the wind sort of blowing her piss toward Karina, the poor thing, who had to jump out of the way to avoid it. At that point we realized something was happening to Ana, but we had soroche and knew that if we walked a little farther, we'd get to a rest stop where we could chew coca or something, alpaca style. It didn't make sense to go back down, no matter how dizzy we were. Anyway, I wanted to turn away like Kari and Nicole to give Anita her privacy, you know? But something came over me, I don't know what, maybe the altitude, and I couldn't stop staring at her butt cheeks. If you've watched the video, you understand how ugly they are. I tried to think about the exercise routine I'd suggest for her to lift those floppy, rectangular buns—you know?—about good things for her and not the stains or cellulitis. And that gave me courage: I questioned why Ana was doing it, peeing like that, like a little pig. Why she didn't take care of herself. Why she'd let herself be filmed. Why she always wanted to be the victim and feel bad instead of doing something for herself. Why she didn't solve her problems instead of wallowing in her difficulties. Seriously, don't get me wrong, but for a few seconds I understood her ex-husband. It was only for a few seconds, you know? And then whatever had come over me was gone.

KARINA

I've been thinking about it a lot these days, about why I turned around so I wouldn't see Ana peeing. Dear, I'm the type of person who wants to understand the little reasons behind their own behavior. I want to know myself better than anyone: to know where my primal urges come from, what wild part of me acts before my will does. The mind is quicker than conscious thought, which is why I write: to trap thought. It sounds good, doesn't it? I've said that in a few interviews. Whatever it was, I looked away, uncomfortable. I turned my back on Ana. But where did that discomfort come from? For Nicole, who is as much a goody two-shoes as can be, it was an understandable reaction. Coming from me, though, it was totally unexpected. I'm going to tell you the truth now that there's trust between us: I turned around not out of modesty but rejection. The video was fresh in my mind, and I didn't want to see Ana's body. It's awful to say, I know. Human emotions are awful most of the time. I was feeling dizzy and nauseous, and I really didn't want to disrupt my view of that beautiful mountain landscape with a crass, unpleasant one. I didn't want to see Ana's body. That's the truth. I think she knew and was testing us. We all failed, of course. Can I have a drag? Thank you, dear. The trail was clear. On the way up we didn't see a soul aside from those brief seconds when we saw an indio in the distance, higher up, looking down at us with a red poncho and wooden walking stick. I'm telling you about it now because when Ana leapt, the indio did the same thing. It was as if the two were the same person, just in different sectors of the mountain. It'll seem crazy to you, but I'd almost swear I saw the indio running in reverse. My blood froze. I saw the end of it all, of course, and couldn't do anything. Maybe it was the soroche. Well, what I mean is that we failed Ana because once again we made her feel bad about herself and her body. She was peeing; it wasn't anything all that shocking. We reacted poorly. I feel guilty for having turned around, for having given in to that emotion unbecoming of the affection I have for her. Above all because if I hadn't done it, I could've stopped her, but as I turned my back on her I only saw the end, when Ana and the indio leapt. A condor? Who told you that, dear?

NICOLE

I don't like to lie; I never do. I lead with the truth, so you can trust me when I tell you: Kari is a liar. And I don't know why, when there's no need. Everything that happened was really sad, really sad, but it obviously wasn't our fault. And if we had to single out a guilty person, it would be Anita's ex, not us, of course. It's a relief she's now safe and healthy with her family. We go almost every day to see her, and we've prayed for her recovery at church because, despite everything, she's our sister, and surely God in His infinite compassion will forgive her. I pray for that! Amen. The thing is, I'd like to say something else, but Kari is a liar: she didn't turn around like she says she did, and there was no indio. It's difficult to explain just like that, look, I'll draw it out for you on a napkin. This was the layout: me here, Anita here, Vivi here, Kari here. See? Even though I had my back to Anita, I could see the others perfectly. I'm the only one who turned around. Vivi thinks Kari turned around with me because she saw her avoid a few drops of pee the wind carried in her direction, but she didn't; she only moved to here, and Vivi couldn't see her anymore. Therefore, the two must have seen Ana pull up her pants and run toward the cliff. I heard screams, nothing more. When I turned back around there was no trace of Anita, and Vivi and Kari's faces were pure horror. The situation embarrassed me. Embarrassed me for them. To do something like that in front of your friends! And then dread, yes, because I thought she'd killed herself. Our dear God never would have forgiven her! If you ask me, I think Kari invented the thing about the indio to justify why she'd moved closer to Vivi instead of grabbing Ana. What I did see was a condor, but just for a few seconds. Beautiful creature. Eerie, but beautiful.

ANA

Listen to me closely, kid, because I'll only say it once. I was pissing on the rocks like an animal of the highlands because that's what I am, a creature that urinates on what is beautiful. They'd been talking about Angelina Jolie, how gorgeous she used to be and how emaciated she is now; about how sad it is to have been perfect only to no longer be so, like a withering rose, like a stream drying up; about how fragile perfection is; about how fleeting youth is; about how such succulent lips can turn into two skinny guajillo peppers; about the skeletal frame of her once voluptuous body, once desired, once loved, and I felt hatred. Yes, a deep hatred for every one of them, for their stupid topics of conversation, for their three-cent opinions, for feeling sorry for me and taking me on a pity trip, but most of all for myself. I hated myself plain and simple. With a rabid honesty. And so I pulled down my pants and peed just like a bitch taken out for a walk, because why not, if I was a pet to them. And I hated the beautiful clouds and the lush mountains and the flowers and the city below, and in that moment, I knew my role in this landscape was to piss my way to death. Get it? Because beauty is my enemy. And I wept, but out of extreme hatred. I wept over the cordillera and Nicole's holier-than-thou back and Viviana and Karina's disgusted, condescending looks. And so, with my ass out in the mountain wind, I assumed for the first time the true form of my existence... Young man, I'm not sure if you know, this only happens once in a lifetime. A revelation so sorrowful that the mind makes it quick, but for me it lasted too long. When you're up so high, you think it will be difficult to see clearly, but that's not true. You clearly see what you are and what others are, how everything below is small and miserable and that is where you come from. This is the true altitude sickness. This is what makes you run. And you see the impossible, and it doesn't matter whether it's real or a hallucination: an indio transforming into a giant condor that casts a shadow upon the day, and you recall the legend. You remember that a condor chooses the moment of his death. That when he feels old, finished, without a mate, he jumps off the highest mountain and onto the rocks. A condor with soroche. And I knew, as I watched the indio's metamorphosis, that to die after taking a piss on the future could be my ultimate act of dignity. So I did it, kid. I folded my wings and failed.

HACÍA AÑOS NO TOMABA
LA SALIDA DEL SUR.

IN THE MOUNTAINS

LINA MUNAR GUEVARA
TRANSLATED BY ELLEN JONES

It's been years since I took the south exit. I've hated it ever since I was little because of the mountains. I know I lost something there, something important, but I can't remember what. This is impossible, because I almost never go to the mountains, but it's true. It's always been true. I tell myself repeatedly that it's impossible, that this is just what happens when you're part of this family.

I think I might have had a chance of being normal if my grandad hadn't grown up in the house with the facing mirrors. Those mirrors in the dining room where, long before he understood what a reflection was, he was forced to see himself repeated not once, not twice, but thousands of times over. Thousands of copies with no beginning and no end. You'd think he'd have taken the mirrors down when he inherited the house, but not only did he leave them there, he also forbade us from touching them. A mandate, he warns, that must outlive him.

"No one's to cover them and no one's to touch them," he says whenever we call him, as though the mirrors weren't there in his own house. Grandad's sick and can't remember our names, but he remembers the mirrors all right.

"No one's to cover them and no one's to touch them." He's scared of them. He's never said so, but you can tell. That's why we never use the dining table in his house, always the kitchen table.

"Grandad's going to die this week," Mom announced, but when I said we should go and see him she replied that it was too late. She's always said she can smell death, that it smells like daffodils, and that by the time she smells them it's too late.

The road heading west was closed. If there had been any other way to get to Grandad's, I would have taken it. I hate the south exit because I don't like the mountains. The road's really windy, and you feel like you're getting nowhere because of the fog. There's no beginning and no end to the mountains. The road is narrow and you can't see anything. The lights of another car seem to blink up ahead. I speed up a bit and see that it's another gray car, like mine, but the fog soon swallows it up until I can't see it anymore.

"Juana's scared of the mountains," Manuel used to say, obnoxiously, when I'd cry before getting into the car. And Dad would scold him because brothers and sisters are supposed to love each other. He lost his brother when he was twenty years old. Uncle Guillo died wearing a mustard-colored shirt and a brown hat. Dad used to tell us how, when they were teenagers, Uncle Guillo had a girlfriend he would visit by riding his bike down a narrow path. One day, after visiting her, my uncle came home looking pale. When asked what had happened, he said he had bumped into a man on the path coming in the other direction on a bike. He said he was wearing a mustard-colored shirt and a brown hat and that when he saw him up close he realized it was himself. Grandma said that everyone looks the same at night. No one thought anything of the story until, years later, Uncle Guillo died on that same path, wearing a mustard-colored shirt and a brown hat.

The headlights reflect off the silver railing along the edge of the road. Up ahead, there's a spot where the railing is completely twisted, destroyed. A car must have driven through it, a car that then disappeared over the cliff. I don't look down into the valley too often; I'm afraid I'll see Uncle Guillo in his mustard-colored shirt, tipping his brown hat in greeting.

"Juana's scared of the mountains." But that's the problem: I'm not scared of them, and I should be. I know I should be scared, because I lost something there and I don't remember what. Grandad's always been scared of getting trapped in the mirrors in the dining room. He's never said so, but you can tell.

Grandma prays for him a lot. She prays for him more than she talks to him. Not just now that he's sick, she always has.

Grandma prays to the Virgin Mary because she's scared of her. She says that, when she was eleven, the Virgin visited her in the creek where she was playing. "At first I didn't know who she was." It was a woman all in white. She felt a breeze turn her legs to ice, but the trees weren't moving. Nothing was moving, not even the creek. She knew the woman had been watching her all her life, since forever. The Virgin smiled and gestured for her to approach. Grandma followed. She would have drowned if some fishermen hadn't jumped in to save her. Grandma didn't go back to the creek.

Behind me, a car flashes its high beams on and off. In the mirror it looks like another gray car. I slow down, but it doesn't catch up. The lights disappear. At the next bend, there's a gap in the railing where a car has slid through, another gray car that's flipped over the cliff. I can't be sure whether I really saw it because when I look down the fog has covered it over.

"No one's to cover them and no one's to touch them." Maybe someone covered the mirrors in the dining room— that's it. Maybe it smells like daffodils because Grandad's died.

The problem is that I like the mountains even though I shouldn't.

Up ahead, the gray car reappears. It comes in and out of

sight. It disappears for a second and I speed up a little to make it reappear. As the bend approaches, I flash my high beams in warning. I hear it skid and crash. I hear metal on metal, glass shattering, and suddenly there's the taste of blood on my lips. When I get around the bend, there is no car, and the railing is intact. I see it coming, but I don't want to brake.

I like the mountains. I always have. I know I shouldn't like them because there's something I'm looking for here, something important, and I can't remember what.

THE

CUANDO EDUARDO
APARECIÓ NO DIJO
DÓNDE ESTUVO...

THIRD

TRANSFORMATION

MAXIMILIANO BARRIENTOS
TRANSLATED BY TIM GUTTERIDGE

WHEN EDUARDO APPEARED, HE DIDN'T SAY WHERE HE'D BEEN, and the people in town assumed he'd spent three days on drugs and had lost all notion of time, wandering around the woods listening to the devil's music. They searched for him relentlessly, even at night. I remember his mother's cracked voice calling out for him. I was the only one who knew he'd gone to the Helmut place.

I saw the old man, he told me on the riverbank where we used to fish on Sunday afternoons, a week after he reappeared.

That's impossible, if he was still living he'd be 110.

They keep him alive, Eduardo went on. He was stuck to the wall, connected to some tubes that came out of these things that looked like flowers.

What are you talking about?

The heat was unbearable, my clothes were soaked in sweat, and my eyes were stinging. The steam rising from the rocks and the trees clouded my sight. We'd spent our lives in that lunar landscape that expanded time, imposing it on us like some limitless viscosity.

He spoke, his voice was in my head, Eduardo said.

I rested a hand on his left shoulder, but he shrugged me off. For the first time since his return his eyes filled with something other than apathy.

We agreed to go together, he said.

You must've dreamed it.

He placed his finger on my forehead and pressed.

His voice was in here, he said.

After that conversation, we stopped being friends. His mother asked me if we'd argued; she asked why I no longer visited and I lied, claiming that between my work and my studies I had no time, that I would come over when I was less busy, that I'd be around next weekend. She was still a beautiful woman, and she looked at me in desperation, as if her son still hadn't fully returned and she hoped I could do something about it.

As soon as school was over, I left town to study law at university. I returned two years later, the summer my father sold the land and the house and my parents moved to the city at my mother's insistence. Eduardo was working on the Ramírez ranch. I bumped into him in a bar. We greeted each other coolly. He was with one of the daughters of Liborio, the

Ramírez family's head cattle herder. The woman led him to one of the tables at the back in the gloom, and I stayed where I was, sitting at the counter, watching them walk away.

It was his mother who got in touch with me after twenty-two years in which I'd had no news of them. She called one morning when I was at the office and about to seal a deal with some Brazilian soy farmers. I don't know how she got my number, but I recognized her voice; it only took me a few seconds. The same voice she'd had back then, when she was a beautiful widow who didn't give in to the advances of the ranchers.

It's Eduardo, he's in a coma, she said.

I took a few steps around my desk and raised my hand to the back of my neck; something was pulsing there.

What happened? I asked.

We don't know. A few days ago he was talking about you. He said he had a notebook he wanted to give you.

...

He was going to call you.

I closed the office door and sat on the desk. Through the window that looked out into the corridor, I saw people walking; I saw their lips moving but couldn't hear what they were saying. I listened to the breathing of this woman who came from a world that until then I thought had disappeared.

We haven't seen each other for ages, I said.

He'll have had his reasons. I don't know if he's going to make it.

What notebook?

One with drawings. You must remember that he drew.

...

I understand if you're not interested or you're too busy, she added before hanging up.

I drove out there early one Saturday morning, three days after receiving that phone call. It had been raining heavily since midnight. The headlights of the approaching cars gleamed and then faded seconds later, violently blotting out the world. Space, during my return journey, was an extension of my memory. As I continued, my memory fused with the rain and the trees, with the clouds charged with electricity and the stubby hills. The movement was physical but also mental. I was moving along the road, but I was also returning to the place in my body where I preserved vestiges of an extinct world: that morning I was still the insecure metalhead, pathologically unsociable, who hated everyone whose life was different from his.

I turned up the volume of *In the Sign of Evil* and thought about the Helmuts, that family of Germans who had arrived in the Chaco in the early 1950s. People told stories about the old man: that he'd been a Nazi, that he'd tortured Guaraní girls in the cellar of the huge farmhouse, that he'd buried the bodies on his land. Nobody ever knew what had happened to him. He'd disappeared at the start of the '70s; he stopped visiting the stores and the bars, and people assumed he'd died and that his only son, who'd married a woman he had brought there from the city, had buried him on the farm.

The old German appeared in our dreams, even though we had never seen him before; he'd died four years before Eduardo and I were born. The first time we talked about it was when we were listening to some CDs that had just arrived from the city—every so often they sent them by bus—it could have been *Transilvanian Hunger* by Darkthrone or *Ceremony of Opposites* by Samael. Our adolescent years passed between the credo of distortion and the ostracism of a small town where we were deemed devil worshippers. People crossed to the other side of the street when they saw us, and if it hadn't been for the respect they had for my father, they would have found a reason to lynch us.

Eduardo said he'd heard him singing in a dream. He didn't manage to see his face, but he was sure the figure in a German army officer's uniform was the old man. After that we became obsessed: we asked our parents to tell us stories, but they repeated the same things we'd already heard, nothing new to feed our morbid curiosity.

He'd come up with the idea of snooping around the farm-house in search of clues. The night we'd agreed to go I lost my nerve. The next day, Eduardo didn't show up to school, and that afternoon people organized a search.

Sodom's riffs were pulsing in the muscles of my neck that rainy morning as I drove at sixty miles an hour, an adrena-line pump that stopped me from falling asleep as I hurtled down that road with no bends. I had met old Helmut's son and his children. A girl who would have been a year or two younger than us. Small dark eyes, fair straw-colored hair, skin so white it was as if it had never seen the sun. Twin boys impossible to tell apart, who never spoke to anyone, who didn't go to school. When they appeared in the street on Sundays as the family went to buy provisions, people stopped whatever it was they were doing and stared at them without any pretense.

The town was unrecognizable. The houses spread across the plain in no particular order, most with exposed-brick façades. Asphalt streets and shops and karaoke bars and stalls with pirated DVDs and repair shops displaying the skeletons of old trucks and hairdressers' and brothels disguised as massage parlors. Hotels with the names of foreign chains, usurped without any fear of reprisals.

The rain had stopped an hour ago, and the damp air alleviated the heat, entering my lungs and filling me with a strange optimism. I wound down the window and drove slowly, observing three women arranging their goods on the sidewalk and shouting at each other in Quechua.

Before heading to Eduardo's mother's house, I went by my old place. My parents had sold it to a couple from Villamontes. I struggled to recognize it because they'd painted it bright yellow and added a second floor.

I got out of the car and just stood there for a few minutes not doing anything until a man came out and asked if I needed something.

I'm good, I said.

I started up the engine and left without giving any explanation.

We went through to the living room. She offered me coffee, and after we'd sat in silence for several long seconds avoiding eye contact, I asked her what the doctors had said.

They didn't find anything. They can't explain what happened, she said.

Why don't you take him to the city?

Eduardo's mother lifted the cup to her lips and took a sip. I didn't understand how she could just accept the situation like that. I found her passivity and resignation unbearable, completely different from that woman I'd known in the late '90s who had organized the search when her son didn't come home. I tried to find, in the face of this old woman, traces of the widow that half the town had once fantasized about, but the only thing I could see clearly was defeat.

Where is he? I asked.

Here. In his room.

He was in a single bed, not connected to monitors or any machines or anything. He seemed to be asleep. She had covered him with an old quilt, which struck me as odd given the heat. His stubble was getting longer and had spread across his cheeks and down his neck. He was almost bald. There was a scar on his chin, perhaps from work one afternoon when he was herding cattle, or else from a fight. I remembered the last time I'd seen him, he'd been with that woman. He had disappeared into the darkness, already drunk, while she laughed at something he'd said that I didn't manage to hear. He had no fingernails.

When she realized that was what I was looking at, his mother said:

They fell out, one by one.

Was it because of what happened?

The doctors didn't see any link.

...

His teeth too, she said.

She held his jaw and parted his lips, inserting two fingers. His breathing was labored and noisy. His blackened gums, ruined from years of chewing coca leaves, lacked teeth. But there weren't any gaps or marks where they'd been pulled out.

Shit, I said, and I looked up at the woman, unable to hide my disgust.

I realized he didn't have any teeth when I found him that morning, she said.

He lost them a long time ago, I said, pointing out the absence of any incisions. His gums were like a baby's. Sealed. Where are they? I added. If someone pulled them out there should have been blood everywhere. When you found him, his clothes must have been a mess.

He was sleeping as calmy as he is now. There was nothing to see. Eduardo was withdrawn. Ever since he reappeared all those years ago, he's never been the same.

...

You knew where he'd been, she said. You always denied it, but you knew what happened to him.

...

You know something you never wanted to tell me. You

were always together; the two of you were the only crazy fans of that devil's music. You were inseparable, but when he returned you stopped seeing each other.

We were going to go to the Helmut place, I said. We wanted to see inside the farmhouse.

It was the first time I'd said it out loud. The confession didn't bring relief as I'd imagined it would. I didn't feel anything, apart from the same indifference that had accumulated over the years.

Why? she asked.

Things you do when you're a kid. We were obsessed with old Helmut, with all the stories that were going around. I guess we wanted to discover something that would corroborate what people said about him.

That's where my son was all those days we were looking for him? You knew and you never said anything?

The only time we talked about it, after his return, Eduardo was rambling, saying things that were hard to believe.

What things?

Things about the old man. Things he saw. He probably dreamed them.

Why didn't you say anything? Why did you make us waste our time?

I thought I might get in trouble. I was seventeen. What was I supposed to do?

You faggot.

She let out a laugh. Wrinkles appeared on her forehead and around her eyelids. Her decrepitude had taken on a life of its own. Her laughter was revolting, the lament of a wounded animal.

Do you know what happened to the Helmuts? she asked once she had composed herself, her face flushed and exuding the same cold resignation she had shown since opening the door of her home.

I don't know anything about the people here.

Now you're living it up in the city you're not interested in us lot.

That's not true.

The two boys died, she said. Do you remember the twins?

When was that?

In 2000.

How did they die?

The house caught fire; they were trapped inside. The father and the girl were in town, buying provisions. They came back to find the place in flames.

And the mother?

She'd walked out on them a year before, left town. She never came back; we never saw her again.

Eduardo's mother sat on a chair beside his bed. She crossed

her legs, and I saw her calves marked by thick veins, her solid dirty feet, and this decrepit woman imposed herself on the memories that involuntarily came to my mind. Of her in her forties—still beautiful, her full lips always painted red—serving us tea, asking us to turn it down, laughing because she couldn't understand why we spent whole afternoons arguing about bands whose names she couldn't pronounce and whose music she couldn't distinguish from noise. The resentment had accumulated over the years and gradually settled in her body, so that now she no longer even used it to hurt others. She wasn't trying to provoke me when she called me a faggot, when she laughed at me for something that had happened more than two decades ago.

Do the father and the girl still live on the farm? I asked.

She shook her head.

They left a year after the tragedy, she said. Maybe they went to look for the mother, maybe they went to the city, or maybe they left the country altogether.

I put my ear to Eduardo's chest. It was as if he had six lungs; his breathing was deafening. I closed my eyes and saw a Mustang—those planes the gringos flew during the Second World War—exploding in the sky. The flames grew, expanded, changed color.

I jumped back, terrified, and almost collapsed in a heap. I

went out into the yard and leaned against a tree, one that had previously held a swing.

You saw something, his mother said.

What?

You saw something.

I wiped the sweat from my neck and shook my head.

They're dreams, she said. If you get close enough you can see them. I've seen them too.

I didn't go back to the city that evening. I booked a room at a hotel that went by the name of El Hilton, called my wife, and told her I was staying on for the weekend. She asked if something had happened, and I told her I was going to take a couple of days to look around town. We'd been together for less than a year.

After we'd hung up, I leafed through the notebook, the kind the ranchers used for their accounts. Drawings, most of them old, maybe the ones he did when he was a kid: the covers of some of the albums we used to love—*To Mega Therion* by Celtic Frost, *Storm of the Light's Bane* by Dissection, *Hvis Lyset Tar Oss* by Burzum. Drawings of teeth, molars, incisors. Some of them were intact, but others were cracked, as if they'd been struck with a hammer. Drawings of flowers with tubes emerging from them: I remembered what he'd told me at the river, when he said he'd seen the old man connected to the wall of that cellar.

Why did he want me to have this notebook? I hadn't seen him in over twenty years. When we stopped speaking to each other I thought he was lying, assumed he'd made it up so I'd feel like a shit for not going with him to the Helmut place. I even suspected he'd never even been to the farm and that he'd fabricated his disappearance to teach me a lesson. Three days wandering around in the woods just to make me feel like a fake.

I put the notebook on the bed, lay down, and closed my eyes. The image of the Mustang exploding in the sky reappeared. I could see every detail as if I were watching a movie. The fire couldn't be contained by my skull; it returned to the world.

When I opened my eyes, I saw Eduardo; he was standing in the hotel room. It wasn't the man in a coma but the kid who'd been my friend. He was wearing his old Kreator T-shirt, faded from use. He was thin, and his hair, long and black and greasy, came down to his shoulders. He was terrified. Although he didn't say anything, his eyes were sick with fear.

Eduardo, I said.

He retreated and cowered against the wall. The room smelled of raw meat. I had to cover my nose. When he disappeared, the smell lingered in the air, the same smell as at the butcher's shop.

They're dreams, I remembered his mother's words. *If you get close enough you can see them.*

On Sunday morning after breakfast, I drove out to the Helmut place. It was raining heavily and visibility was poor. In almost an hour I hardly met another vehicle. I put on *In the Sign of Evil* and drove at top speed. Out of nowhere, a deer appeared with its young.

I managed to swerve and brake.

I got out.

The deer stood looking at me for a few seconds then disappeared into the woods, followed by its offspring. Adrenaline was pulsing fiercely in my neck. I didn't care about getting wet. I put my hand on the fender; if it hadn't been for my reflexes, it would have been covered with blood. I would probably have been dead. I looked at the windshield and saw my skull and the hair and the blood that were no different from those animals'.

I came to the main entrance to the Helmut farm. There were no tracks and I guessed nobody had visited the place for a while. The dirt road was a quagmire. The foundation was still solid. The timber was charred, whipped by the rain. I turned off the engine but didn't get out. The deer I'd almost run over reappeared in my mind, its glassy eyes reminding me of Eduardo's, the same terrified look as when he appeared in my hotel room.

I walked around the perimeter of what had once been the Helmut farm. There was just burnt timber and debris, broken furniture, and delicate vegetation taking over what had once been walls. The place hadn't even been looted; it was thought to be cursed and had been preserved like a shrine to some ancient tragedy.

I sat down and watched the rain fall on the roof of the car that I'd parked a few yards away. The sky was blotted out by gray clouds that lost their shape as they expanded and merged with one another. I walked around the rubble and, behind what might have been a huge sideboard where the dishes and crockery were kept, discovered the door to the cellar. I turned on the flashlight on my cellphone and went down.

It smelled of rotten meat.

When I reached the bottom of the stairs, I saw the drawings on the walls. Children's drawings. I assumed they'd been done by the twins, who spent most of their time alone in a house that lacked electricity or any modern distractions. Trees and cars and the façades of some of the stores in town, I recognized the Hernández's pharmacy and the Sullivans' hardware store. Drawings of the sister, a girl almost in her teens, and of the father and the mother.

I tripped on a brown tube; it looked like a piece of intestine. I illuminated one of the walls and found the drawing of two metalheads. They had long hair, black T-shirts.

It was us.

Eduardo and me.

I parked in front of his mother's house and knocked on the door until she opened up.

I went to the Helmut place, I said.

She showed me in. We went through to the living room and had coffee.

What the hell happened to Eduardo? I asked.

...

When I told you he'd been to the farm when he disappeared, you already knew.

...

He went back, didn't he? Before he fell into a coma, he went back.

...

That whole performance, the laughter, the accusations, it was just for show. You knew where your son had been.

He dreams through my son, she said after a while, still retaining that docility that was neither resignation nor tiredness, and which was far more intimidating than if she had threatened me directly.

They change the place, she added. The dreams modify it.

She went to the kitchen and returned with a lit cigarette hanging from her lips.

What are you talking about?

The second transformation has already begun, she said, and she pointed to the room where her son was.

What are you saying?

Angélica told me this would happen. She was the one who gave me your number, the one who asked me to call you. She convinced me of Eduardo's mission.

She rubbed the back of her neck and blew the smoke out through her nose.

Which Angélica?

The oldest daughter, she said. The one who was saved from the fire.

She took another draw and blew more smoke out through her nostrils. Her hair was tied up: white, it contrasted with the green of her eyes, the only thing that seemed to resist the aging process.

Do you want to see him?

She went into the room where Eduardo was.

Come, she said from inside.

Through the window I saw my car. I could leave and forget about everything. For twenty-two years I had kept my distance from what went on in this town. I'd established my own life, married a beautiful woman I'd met at a friend's wedding, which had been canceled because the bride got cold feet at the last minute. Alejandra was one of the bridesmaids; we got drunk at a bar with some guests who were still in a state of shock and embarrassment. I could leave, get away, turn all this madness into a dream, something I would avoid speaking about, something I would carry on denying until I had forgotten it altogether.

It's beautiful, Eduardo's mother said. You have to see it.

I stood up and went into the bedroom. The walls were covered with delicate vegetation, similar to that covering the rubble at the Helmut place. At first I thought they were insects, little moths, but when I got closer I saw that what was sprouting from the down that covered the ceiling and the door were incisors and molars. Teeth encircling huge tropical flowers that looked like toads, from which emerged the tubes I had found on the cellar floor, the tubes Eduardo had drawn in the notebook.

Touch them, his mother said.

They smelled of raw meat, the same smell that had saturated the hotel room when Eduardo had materialized in the air then vanished seconds later.

What are these?

She tore one off and handed it to me: red with white threads like the veins of fat in a piece of bacon. The texture was rough, like a cow's stomach.

They're made of meat, I said.

She inhaled smoke and blew it out through her nostrils, just like she had in the living room. She scrutinized me with those eyes of hers, so green and inexpressive.

Everything you see here is his dream, she said.

The tubes that emerged from the flowers were crisscrossed with fine blue arteries.

He dreams through Eduardo, she said. They modify the place; the room is his body now. When the third transformation happens, he's going to emerge from there, and she pointed at her son.

Who?

Old Helmut, she said. This is his dream.

She approached the bed and pulled back the quilt that covered Eduardo's body. He was naked, the skin of his chest covered with the same delicate green vegetation. Teeth sprouted around his navel.

He's going to flower, she said.

What have you done to me?

She wanted me to call you, she said you had to return.

This is madness, I said, and I took a few steps back and looked at the door, which was still open.

He's watching us, she said.

The breathing was coming from the flowers. They filled the room, rarefying the air.

You've drugged me, I said. All this shit I'm seeing is in my head. I can't get out of my head. I have to get out of my head.

They're going to dream through you too, she said.

What?

The boys are going to come back.

She grabbed one of the tubes and held it up. With a rapid movement, she held my jaws firmly, pressed, and connected it to the back of my neck. I felt a stabbing pain and everything went black. The room, the foul-smelling flowers, the sunlight that entered through the only window: it all disappeared.

The blackness lasted a few seconds.

And then I saw them.

The twins were in the bed in my room, in the house that Alejandra and I had just bought. My wife hugged them as if they were her children. Her laughter mingled with the laughter of the boys, who were just as I remembered them.

Come here, she said. Don't be afraid.

It wasn't her voice; it was her body but not her voice.

You aren't Ale, I said.

She whispered something to the twins and asked me to come closer again, told me not to be afraid. She stretched out an arm toward me, but I stayed still. I tugged at the tube; I wanted to rip it out, but the pain was so intense that it was too much for me. There was blood on my fingertips.

They're going to grow inside your body, said the woman who seemed to be my wife. They're going to flower, she said. That will be your gift. You're going to bring them back to me.

One of the twins undid her nightdress and put a nipple in his mouth. I felt a pain in my neck, a jolt; he was sucking through the tube.

Suddenly I was back in the room with Eduardo, and his mother was laying me into a bed next to her son's. She undressed me. She put my pants on a chair, on top of my folded T-shirt. She took off my underwear and put them with the rest of my clothes. I wanted to scream at her, to tell her to stop, but I couldn't open my mouth.

A woman entered the room. Blonde, pale. Tiny black eyes, as small as a bird's. Her hair was dull. The last time I had seen her she'd been a teenager; I remembered seeing her in the back of a truck that her father was driving. She was surly, shy, unable to hold a man's gaze.

He's resisting, Eduardo's mother said.

The vegetation was growing on my chest. It was tearing open my pores, emerging from my rectum, from my anus: I felt it spreading across my buttocks and climbing up my back until it reached Eduardo's body.

They were sucking, I could feel it in my neck. The twins were feeding.

I tried to stand up but my legs didn't respond; I had no will. My body had ceased to belong to me.

Don't struggle, Angélica said. It will be pointless and painful.

It was the same voice as Alejandra's when she'd hugged the twins. She brought her face close to mine—her bird's eyes, black, almost things—and closed my eyelids.

VISITOR

JULIÁN ISAZA
TRANSLATED BY JOEL STREICKER

LA NOCHE EN QUE SE DESENCADENARON LOS
EXTRAÑOS EVENTOS, ME ENCONTRABA LEYENDO
EN LA POLTRONA QUE TENGO FRENTE A MI VENTANA.

THE NIGHT THAT WOULD UNLEASH THE STRANGE SERIES OF events, I was reading in an easy chair in front of my window. I'm a voracious reader, and once I'm done with my household chores—cleaning, making lunch, and watering the plants in the garden—I devote the rest of the day to my books until well after dark. That warm evening, I was immersed in the fascinating story of the inhabitants of Atlantis and their relationship to visitors from other worlds, a subject that has intrigued me for some time: how they built the Egyptian pyramids, created the Bermuda Triangle, and made the strange signs that have appeared in wheat fields throughout the world. That's why, reflecting on everything in hindsight, I can't be sure that the unusual event was completely random, although I can't say that I was chosen, either. What I can state, without a doubt, is that since then my tranquil existence has been covered in a sinister cloak.

I had my feet up, as recommended to promote blood circulation, and was reading my book when an intense flash lit up the sky, as if one of the many stars punctuating the firmament's darkness had exploded. I, who have always been a nervous woman, was petrified. A second later the orange trees outside shook violently, and the windowpanes rattled with such force that it seemed incredible they didn't break.

I couldn't even shout. I was frozen. Anyone seeing me just then, muscles rigid, eyes popping—showing the unmistakable signs of rigor mortis—would have concluded that I was dead. But I was still alive, very much alive: I could feel my heart in my mouth. I don't know exactly how long I was like that, but after a while I began to move cautiously, with as much stealth as this old sixty-seven-year-old body allows.

I went out to the garden and, finding myself under the cloak of night, turned on an outside light. There was a fresh, gentle breeze. I made my way forward—not without fear—to inspect for damage to my plants and hopefully find some clue that would explain what had just happened. Still, I didn't come across anything but unsettled leaves and branches. I took a deep breath and started considering the most obvious hypotheses. My first thought was that it'd been lightning, but I discarded that theory upon seeing that the sky was completely clear. Then I thought it might have been a short circuit in one of the electrical towers, but that notion dissolved upon noting that the lights in my house were still on. I was deep in these musings when I heard a sound, like the weak rustling of dry grass. I figured that the best thing to do would be to go back inside right away and seek refuge, but curiosity got the better of me, and my trembling legs carried me forward in the direction of the sound.

As I got closer, my eyes could make out the shapes in the half-light a little better. Back there, a few meters away, I discovered a small figure lying on the ground in the fetal position. Whatever it was, it looked pretty defenseless. It was barely moving. I observed the creature for a few seconds, but it was hard to tell what it was. I reached out my hand in the hope that touching it would give me a clue. My fingertips rested on what could have been its back. Its skin felt soft. The small being shook, but it didn't put up any resistance, so I bent down and picked it up. It was extremely light, as if it didn't have any organs or bones inside. As soon as I had it in my arms, I felt what could have been its hand gripping one of my fingers like a newborn, although I was sure it wasn't human and didn't belong to this world. And that certainty both terrified and filled me with joy because, somehow, this poor old woman had been given the privilege of being part of an exceptional encounter.

I took it inside and examined it. It was a little more than two feet long. Its head was very big, with two enormous eyes. Its arms were long, slim, and very smooth, as if they didn't have any joints, which its legs seemed to lack, too: they were lax and hingeless. It reminded me right away of an old toy my son had, a Kermit the Frog that I still have stored with some of his other belongings, tucked away in a box in what used to be his room. Its anatomy called attention to its overall fragility. And its skin was strange, green and elastic, like an amphibian's.

It stared at me with very black eyes. In fact, they were mostly pupil. It looked at me as if it were studying me, but also with an expression of profound helplessness. That made sense because it seemed so exhausted, so sick, or so wounded that it was totally vulnerable. I talked to it, said it could relax because it was in good hands. Although it's likely it didn't understand my words, its body relaxed, and it put its tiny three-fingered hand in mine. Then, a whitish membrane lowered over its eyes.

Because I wouldn't let it sleep in my room (I wasn't that brave), I had to set it up in my son's room. And that's what I did: I tucked it into bed and closed the door. I won't lie: several times I got up, intent on taking the creature out and leaving it in the weeds, but then I retraced my steps, disconcerted by what seemed a cruel and repugnant idea. Getting to sleep was impossible. All manner of thoughts crossed my mind, each one more ludicrous than the last. I thought, for example, about the being's origin. But it was useless to speculate because the answer was out of my reach. I thought then about its intentions, and I was filled with terror. What if it tried to experiment on me? What if it was the first sign of an invasion? What if it came through the door bent on murdering me? I shivered and cursed myself for having taken it in, but I tried to calm myself with the sad realization that, if it were faking its lamentable state and had sinister intentions, what could I, a poor old woman, do to fend it off? Besides, if it was going to attack, surely it would've done so by now.

I watched the night give way to the first rays of morning. I got up, puffy-eyed, tired, and covered in sweat. And the day didn't promise much rest, either. My life, which has always been simple, had been shattered, and now I was sharing my roof with a guest that I both pitied and feared. I walked around the house and checked that everything was just the same, but evidently everything had changed.

I opened the door to my son's room and found that my guest had recovered its strength. With one long hop, just like a batrachian, it hid under the bed. Bending down, I saw only the liquid shine of its enormous eyes, which, cautiously, drew close enough that I could see myself reflected in them. I felt dizzy: its gaze told me nothing. It was inert and enigmatic. I shuffled backward, and the combination of my clumsy feet and my excess weight landed me on the floor. I fell on my back like a beetle, and, while I tried to get up, the creature came out of its hiding place and stood at my side. I couldn't have been any more confused by its sudden presence and couldn't decide whether to keep still or continue backing up. The choice I made was the consequence of a most outlandish act: the small being opened its arms and glued itself—I can't find a more precise word—to my body; I didn't move a muscle until, after a few minutes, it decided to free me.

I avoided that room the rest of the morning. I found myself unsettled—lost, even—in the face of a situation that could only be considered insane. But, as time passed, I began to relax, faced with the reality that my singular companion was here to stay. I even began to worry about it, about its wellbeing.

It wasn't until the afternoon that I realized that the being hadn't eaten. Like every living thing, it would have to consume some type of food, which posed a dilemma of Jurassic proportions and provoked an anguish of similar dimensions. How could I nourish that organism, whose biology was a mystery to me? Could it even digest any Earth food, or would anything I offered it be toxic to its system? There was no way to know, and the only sensible option that occurred to me was letting it indicate which path to take. So, I prepared a tray with a variety of possibilities: a little fruit, raw and cooked meat, vegetables, some cheese, and even a little chicken soup that I'd made myself for lunch, as well as a glass of water.

I set it down before my guest, but nothing drew its attention, much less its appetite, not even the water. In fact, it pursed its lips, demonstrating its evident rejection of what I'd offered it. I could do little but take the tray away and ready myself to leave the creature alone again, but just as I turned my back on it, it put its arms around me again, hugging my leg for fifteen seconds. Then it released me and went off to curl up in a dark corner.

The scene repeated itself over the next few days. Whenever I went into its room, it would emerge suddenly from some nook or cranny and clutch me. Ambushed, I never knew where it would leap out from until it was right on top of me. It was fast enough to become a blur for an instant. Once it let me go, it would calmly turn around and return to its hiding place. It wasn't a hug, it wasn't love, it wasn't even a demonstration of sympathy. It was something else, not so much emotional as practical.

After a while, I discovered what it was. I began to space out my visits to its room to see what effect it might have on its behavior. If I stayed away for an entire day, the next day the creature would be less agile and could no longer easily surprise me. If my absence lasted two days, my little guest wasn't even capable of ambushing me at all. It barely came out of its hiding place, dragging its feet toward me. After three days, I would find it sleeping, in an almost comatose lethargy. The more time that passed, the more fragile it became, and the more avidly it clung to me when it found me again. I concluded that its "embrace" was nothing more than its way of feeding itself and, therefore, that I was its only source of nutrition.

This fact could've worried me, but it didn't, for the following two reasons: First, I felt perfectly fine. I mean, I didn't feel any physical decline or weakening in my health, which is what you'd expect if the relationship were parasitical. Second, my spirits had begun to lift. Ever since my son had left seventeen years ago, I'd become a lonely and sad woman, but this had changed immediately with the arrival of this being who, by the way, I decided to baptize Kermit, given its already-mentioned resemblance to my son's old toy. I loved having company and being responsible for something; it filled my days with activity. In a way, the two of us kept each other alive—it was the perfect symbiotic relationship.

Everything would've continued wonderfully if not for an unexpected turn of events. By that point, Kermit had been with me for a little over two months, and I'd become accustomed to its presence. It no longer unnerved me to discover it spying on me from behind a door, or hear it digging around late at night in the boxes that contained my son's things. That expression that I'd first considered sinister when, in the middle of the night, it would stand next to my bed contemplating me no longer bothered me. Nevertheless, our emerging routine was interrupted by the arrival of another visitor.

I remember clearly that it was raining with such ferocity that it felt like the precursor to the apocalypse. It was as if it were, with the violence of ear-splitting thunder and intense, bluish light, announcing impending doom. Nothing good can happen at such a moment.

Someone knocked on the door. I could barely hear it over the storm's intensity, but soon the knocking got louder. I looked out the window and saw a man with his back to me. A big man dressed in black. Because I never have visitors, I sensed some approaching calamity. Then the knocking turned into pounding—it seemed like they were going to knock down the door—and I decided to open it, first ensuring that Kermit was well hidden.

My son Antonio stood there before my eyes.

It took me a moment to recognize him, not only because he was fatter and balder, but because over the last seventeen years I had seen him only twice, and briefly at that. Once when my mother died, and again when he came for some of his belong-ings. In that entire time, my son had made it his business to avoid me: He didn't call, nor did he take my calls. He didn't visit me, let alone invite me to visit him.

During that time, I often asked myself what I'd done to earn such deep contempt, such cruel indifference. From others I learned that he lived in the city, was successful, married, and had two daughters. Those were bitter years in which I came up with all manner of theories to explain his behavior. I accused myself of all types of crimes, and my mind suffered as much as my body. I had to take all kinds of medicines to ease the pro-found pain that put my health and sanity at risk. In the end, all I was left with was resignation and the occasional bit of informa-tion that came my way. And now here he was, wet, silent, shat-tering the delicate equilibrium that I had created with Kermit.

He entered without saying a word, as if he'd never left, and sat in one of the dining room chairs, leaving a wet, muddy trail behind him. He huffed and drummed his fingers on the table. He looked grave.

"Mom, I'm screwed. I lost everything," he said finally, his voice a whisper.

"Hello, son." I murmured the greeting he wasn't capable of giving me while I observed his back.

For a while, I forgot about the small guest in his room,

and devoted myself to listening to a monologue in which Antonio related that he had lost his job, his wife had asked for a divorce, and his daughters didn't want to see him. He spoke for hours as if he were alone. He cried with his head resting on his arms. I suppose he was waiting for my maternal consolation, which never came because, throughout his litany, I was still holding out hope for even the most minimal expression of apology.

Finally, he dried his tears and I had to—I had to!—offer him his old room. Just then I remembered Kermit. I now faced a series of dilemmas that demanded immediate solutions. Should I tell my son about it? No. It was too risky to reveal such a strange being. And if I didn't introduce the two of them, how would I keep Antonio ignorant of Kermit's existence? The problem required a clever solution, so I told Antonio that I needed a moment to clear out his room, which gave me a chance to hide Kermit in a cardboard box and move it to my room.

I don't know if it was the best idea. From that moment on, Kermit slept by my side and could therefore feed on me all night long. For hours at a time, it stuck to my back, its cold and viscous skin warmed by my body. It clung to me with enough strength that my nocturnal movements didn't uncouple us, and I could feel how it drained me, how the energy transferred from my body to its, to the point where, when I tried, I no longer had the strength to pull it off me.

I had the most unusual dreams. As the nights passed, my brain devoted itself to recreating grotesque situations, to losing itself in scenes that seemed the product of a mind sick with malaria. But despite their outrageousness, the dreams showed a certain sense of continuity, leading me to think that my unconscious wasn't their author, at least not the only one. I dreamed that I gave birth to an immense frog, which I then brought to my breast to nurse. I also dreamed that Antonio was a child again, and he sat at the table to devour a monstrous batrachian, while wearing a crooked and malignant smile. I dreamed about thousands of toads moaning and stretching out their palm-like feet, as if begging for my help. Delirium, pure delirium.

When I woke up, I felt Kermit at my side, and I couldn't tell whether it had been protecting me while I slept or spying on me. Nevertheless, I knew that its physical closeness was no longer necessary for me to feel it. And when I say "feel it," I mean that I perceived it clearly, I understood its desire that we never separate, its intense panic with respect to Antonio, its ambition to encompass me completely.

The few times I left the room, Kermit shot me a resentful look from the darkness. And, to be honest, I wasn't completely pleased about leaving. I became more and more uncomfortable bumping into the ungrateful son that fate had provided me, that man who at this point was a stranger who only used me for the roof I afforded him while he weathered this storm in his life, that man who had the nerve to expect that I feed him but who grunted every time I tried to ask him why he'd abandoned me. That man who was so ashamed of me that he had exiled me from his existence.

A deep and silent chasm opened between us. I confined myself to gritting my teeth, he to ignoring me.

I don't know how long we would've continued like that if Kermit hadn't sent that message, clear—much clearer than any of those cryptic and delirious dreams—and direct to my mind. It was like a flash. At that instant, I was making lunch. I immediately understood what Kermit was suggesting. It was an idea, and the directions to carry it out. Then, without deliberation and guided as if by a superior force, I found myself condimenting the food with a good dose of rat poison. Then I found myself serving the dish, putting it on the table, and calling Antonio.

I knew exactly what would happen, but it was as if I were locked inside my own body, observing everything through a window. I saw my son swallow the food with delight; I saw him convulse; I saw thick foam sprout from his mouth, his veins swollen, his face red. I saw him agonize and I saw myself curled up next to him, holding his head and humming a lullaby. I also saw Kermit leave my room, walking slowly, and sit next to us, like a child who has come to nose around.

For the next three days, I gave myself over to the arduous work of digging Antonio's grave in my garden and burying him. The task was a colossal challenge for a woman my age, but I undertook it with all the devotion that my love as a mother afforded. I even put flowers on the grave and prayed.

Our lives settled into a routine again, with its familiar gentleness: Kermit and I were comfortable, together. Wherever I went, Kermit went. If I went to the bathroom, it followed me. If I went out to take care of my plants, there it was. And I don't think I'm exaggerating if I say that our happiness was almost complete. And I use the word "almost" because even giving my little guest all my attention and loving care, I knew it felt alone and bored.

That's why it occurred to me to give it an inanimate companion, like we do for kids, one that would entertain it. And I thought then that it would be a good idea to give it that old Kermit the Frog toy that had once made Antonio so happy, and that surely would make Kermit even happier, as its extraordinary resemblance to it might serve as a substitute for a companion of its own species. But for all my looking for that toy, for all my turning the house upside down and examining its every corner, I couldn't find it. That unsettled me. Nevertheless, I forget all that, especially when I see it there on the sofa, its legs and arms splayed out in a cross, its mouth open in joy, as if it were waiting for a hug.

THE MAN WITH THE LEG

YO HABÍA CERRADO LOS OJOS MIENTRAS
VIAJÁBAMOS HACIA EL BRONX.

GIOVANNA RIVERO

TRANSLATED BY JOAQUÍN GAVILANO

MY EYES WERE CLOSED AS WE TRAVELED TOWARD THE BRONX.

I enjoy looking at people—their unique faces that I will certainly never see again. I like to guess at their worries and those desires that are not extinguished by the repetition of their daily commutes, the tireless trains, and the abandoned newspapers. But this time, instead of looking, I wanted to feel the rattling, the peripheral electricity of the metallic movement enveloping me like a mother. That's what I wanted: a motherly electricity in that multiparous cavity that advanced with all its creatures to launch them into life. I understood then why terrorists choose trains. It's not just a random assortment of people: it's an intimate and fortuitous filigree of tiny obsessions; minor debts; blue-collared workers; simple, innocent dreams; small-scale selfishness; concealed exhaustion—in short, life in all its raw intensity. All of this, gone in a single explosion.

That's why I didn't notice him. My eyes were closed. I was lost in a dream about my former life—images and voices flitting through my mind. My younger brother, for example, was back to that happy age of four or five. It was the feast of St. John, someone had set up a bonfire in the middle of the yard, and we were playing to see who could hold their finger in the flames the longest. We had a theory about hell. And there too—in that inferno of our fantasies—voices churned, voices speaking unrecognizable languages. Our small fingers began to scorch, roasting like marshmallows. They smelled burned. Yes sir, they did. But we were so happy, just waiting to get down to the bone.

"We're here," my husband said. His voice brought me back to the train, its doors opening efficiently for its usual exchange of creatures. The machinery expelled us and swallowed another swarm of hurried beings who did not have time to think about terrorism and just wanted to nap for the remainder of their trip.

As we reached the surface, stepping out into a neighborhood that oddly mirrored El Alto in Bolivia—sprawling, gray, expansive like a cursed wasteland—my husband turned to me and asked what I'd thought about the man.

"Which man?"

"The man," he said, "the one who got on one stop after

us—I can't believe you slept through it—the man who paraded his stinky leg like someone walking their dog."

"A dog?"

"A rotting dog. He told everyone that his leg was gangrenous and that he didn't have a single peso and couldn't get it amputated." My husband likes to call the gringo quarters "pesos."

"Did you give him money? Did anyone give him money?"

"People don't have time for that," he said, unable to suppress the stress that had been fermenting in his brain for days.

"Time for *that*?" I repeated. I was itching for him to admit that he saw no promise in this getaway of ours. Why were we even in New York? Why hadn't we jetted off to some tropical paradise? The idea of meeting the friends my husband had shared his "dark years" with, as he dubbed them—a period that to me seemed so bright, unrestrained, and authentic—carried with it a danger that I couldn't quite put my finger on. Maybe I was afraid that those dark years would kidnap him, leaving me all alone in this infinite city.

"Better times will come," he sighed, his face softened by grief. Two months ago, I had suffered my third loss—this time not merely a clot, but a complete fetus that reminded us of the poignant creatures we'd once been, that raw mandrake of our origin—and once again I was subjecting myself to another rush of hormones.

I carried a tiny first-aid kit with syringes and little golden bottles around with me, and upon waking up, the first thing I did was inject the "pregnancy elixir" in my thighs (he hadn't explicitly said so, but there was something about this image, more than anything else, that aroused my husband and made our mission less overwhelming, protected by the stubborn ferocity of desire). In any case, it had become normal for me to fall asleep anywhere. And when I woke up, with my nipples becoming erect at the slightest touch, I could feel that it was time for the longed-for fetus to grab some Darwinian willpower and make, for example, from its jaws, a little finger; from its tentacles, plump legs; from its swollen eyes, a look capable of dismantling our most polite lies. It was only natural that such a distressing hypersensitivity would end up rubbing off on my husband. And if you think about it, these hormones that fertilize you like a prairie green cow are like pheromones: you smell them, you inhale them, you metabolize them.

We turned a street corner, guided by only our instincts, looking for a Dominican restaurant that served a nice thick soup that would revive us after the unfamiliar Korean food we had been surviving on for two days in the outskirts of Manhattan. My husband recognized someone up ahead and lowered his voice, even though I was pretty sure the guy wouldn't understand his Spanish, not only because he was a

Black man from the Bronx, but also because he seemed to be too immersed in his own theatrics: "the Man with the Leg..." my husband said.

And there he was, *the Man with the Leg*, leaning against the decapitated neck of what had been a guitar, which now served as a cane. He was singing—or that's how I understood it, fresh to new cultural experiences—he was singing a hoarse blues, hauntingly hopeful.

"When you ain't got no money to cut your leg, your dirty leg, you damn sure you will die soon... So, folks, brothers and sisters, you are seeing now a dead man, isn't it a nightmare? Have mercy and spare me a coin... Save your soul!"

I approached and dropped three quarters into his small tin, then took my time rummaging through my backpack to see if I had one more. I did this while inhaling—as if from a stale but unquestionably authentic perfume—the sour-sweet smell of diseased flesh, flesh that's surrendering, seduced by the unstoppable advances of death. That smell, my God, it put me in a trance. I was disgusted by other things. Specifically, the light, which seemed to be agitating my insides. That anorexic light, that discolored Bronx light, squeezing my esophagus, making me gag.

I found another coin and, rather than dropping it into the can, extended my arm, prompting him to lift his hand. Our fingers grazed; though his body was already succumbing to decay, the man flashed a smile. The striking whiteness of his teeth seemed to weaken death's hold on him.

"God bless you, sista," the man said quietly. I felt a violent condescension in that gratitude; perhaps that final, solitary coin had been a gesture of pity rather than compassion, and the Man with the Leg, with his old heart, could tell the difference, separating the wheat from the chaff without hesitation. "May God repay you with that thing your heart withes for so bad." We walked away as if pursued by his blessing. My husband never likes strangers blessing him; he doesn't want to bear the responsibility of that unnamed, secret impulse, that moral arrogance disguised as piety. (He believes in other traditions, though. Like syringes piercing the skin of my thighs before having deep, blinding, persistent sex, ready to use up every drop of his sperm.)

"Here," said my husband, pulling the hand sanitizer out of his backpack. I complied to avoid getting into a pointless argument based on false concepts and horrible prejudices. Still, I looked at his knuckles, his skin cracked by excessive hygiene, and tried to think like him, keeping his obsessions in mind: I looked around and calculated the invisible threats; the bacteria; the countless ways in which disease enters a body, colonizes it, and then defeats it.

There was the dazzling horror, all those germs in constant bloom. There, the dirty placenta of the world. There too, obscene and neurotic, our insistent desire to have a son, a child that would bind us forever, that would force us to overcome the absurd labyrinths of our respective personalities, a child as a horizon.

Maybe even a daughter. A daughter the better to love.

That night, after returning from a drunken reunion with my husband's friends, we found ourselves slipping into an awkward sexual encounter. We had realized that even his friends had had to face the challenges of adulthood, and those who'd tried to resist were seen as pitiful. We were both looking for an orgasm that would provide us with a few seconds of oblivion, a brief burst of pleasure and its fascinating agony. I added a siren's howl to our rhythmic thrusting, as the buzz of traffic below us boiled with its idiotic happiness. In our five years of marriage, we had repeated this sequence of movements with lust and devotion, in a routine that was far from tedious. The routine played out identically each time, honed to perfection, a legitimate technique: licking, thrusting, pulling his feet up for me to suck, breathing in short gasps as his heavy hand closes around my neck, thumb in my mouth, thrusting back in, pounding the vulva, holding on with my hips, pushing against my clitoris as we finish, kissing his left shoulder as if thanking or betraying him.

Just like that, always the same. Infallible. If I owed any-thing to the breakfast injections it was that, the magnificent alertness of my vagina to squeeze, secrete, hold, suck, drink that juice essential to our mission.

After returning from our short vacation, the doctors would scan each and every follicle to probe how tender and fleshy they had become.

"You're all set," they'd say, and I would feel as full to the brim as the cow in the green pasture.

"Call me Clarabelle," I might even reply.

That night I slept on my back. Despite my drunkenness, I had managed to hoist my legs up against the wall, trying to make whatever was going on in the gloom of my pelvis do so efficiently, in that cellular production far beyond my basic comprehension. It was enough that I'd learned to inject myself meticulously, always hypnotized by the small welt that later formed where the needle had slit the skin. I needed to massage the injected site circularly, which I did while concentrating on the stinging intensity of its burning, praying that my blood would also surrender to that onslaught.

I dreamed about the Man with the Leg. I dreamed that a crowd of people were getting off the subway cars and rushing toward the corner where the man was delivering his mournful sermons that sounded like prophecies to the tune of a rickety blues. Everyone wanted to touch his decomposing leg for a few seconds, closing their eyes and making a wish. The man responded immediately to each person with an answer that they then had to interpret. When it was my turn, I could not touch his leg; the man smiled at me with his gleaming teeth, inviting me to do so. The anguish I felt at not being able to touch that sacred leg was frightening.

I woke up with my heart racing and my legs numb: my feet had slipped from the wall and my knees were bent outward, like a little Buddha defying gravity. The dawn was pouring through the silk curtain of our hotel room. For a while I thought about the huge bank loan we'd gotten in order to carry out our "mission." The tests, the labs, the medical consultations not covered by insurance, the recommended vacations so that those unexpected centers of hormonal, cellular, and muscular performance could be loosened up. Was it really worth it?

As I was peeing, breathing in the acidic mist, the fabulous mixture of semen and that hormonal concoction, I decided that we would go back to the Bronx that afternoon. I wanted to see the Man with the Leg. Never before had I contaminated reality with the delirium tremens that were my dreams. Those two worlds remained separate; but now, perhaps due to the excessive dosage of substances and stimulants inflaming my mucous membranes, I couldn't prevent this incessant manipulation of my body from affecting my real life anymore, demanding some sort of response from it.

Back on the ferry, with the Freedom Tower getting bigger as we grew closer, my husband said he thought it had been a bad idea to have built such a huge thing.

"Sometimes it's best to let things heal on their own," he said. "A flat park full of trees would have been much healthier."

I could think of nothing better than to rediscover the beauty in darkness, the destiny in tragedy. "We wouldn't have met if it hadn't happened," I said slowly, reaching for his cold, cracked hand in his coat pocket. My husband didn't answer; he watched the rippling water for a while, rhythmic, churning, then pointed to the building and smiled.

"I thought all the smoke was coming from the Chinese man's stores," my husband said. "I thought that maybe all the Mexicans he exploited had finally risen up and set fire to either the upper floors, the warehouses, or the entire city." He paused for a moment. "The smoke hung there, you know, for a long, long time, floating around like a soul. Without it, everything would've stunk. I was out of a job anyway. But then Florida came along, and things took the right turn."

My husband has always had the good sense to omit details that might generate uncomfortable connections or cast unnecessary shade. I have always known that this "right turn" is a polite way of acknowledging that his new life is unquestionably more appropriate than the one he had in that tiny apartment with slanted corridors that he shared, perhaps with illusions, with she-who-shall-not-be-named. He never found out what she'd been doing up there that day, burning into smoke and ashes. That hour. There. Collapsing into nothingness. I no longer catch him looking at the images of the bodies disgorged by the disaster; he's replaced those obsessions over time.

I couldn't help but think about the absurdity of my desire as we drove north through the city in search of the Man with the Leg. What exactly was I looking for? We should've returned immediately to our house in the swamps and taken a real vacation, without injections, without the ghosts of the two shores of that city that made me so jealous. I couldn't help but be drawn in by that man's contradictory vitality. So I closed my eyes and let myself be carried away by the magnificent vibrations of the train, which cut through the darkness and tunnels before emerging briefly into the flickering fluorescence of the cityscape.

The Man with the Leg was there, on the same corner. A couple of Rastafarians were chatting with him. We approached slowly; I was paying close attention to the way the smell had intensified, feverish and unforgettable, taking possession of the neighborhood. The Rastafarians were trying to convince the man to go to the county hospital. They could go with him; they had all the time in the world. The man refused, shaking his head gently but firmly. "Oh, perfidious friends, I would never go to a hospital to die like a dog. If I didn't die in the war, like a man, why would I humiliate myself in an emergency room, in such lonely agony?"

The man's will left no room for the Rastafarians' logical but inhumane proposal. Did they really think that throwing him in a cold room with endless rows of sick people and suffering souls would "cleanse" the streets, and absolve them of their postmodern consciences? "Oh, perfidious friends," the man muttered, his head swaying from side to side like a precious pendulum of fixed ideas. The Rastafarians searched through the knots of their own hair for some common sense, then had the decency to ask him what he preferred to do. The leg, covered in grimy blue jeans, gave off an unpleasant odor. *If he died on the street, where would he end up? In a municipal crematorium,* they debated among themselves, their voices passionate like evangelists.

After a long back-and-forth, in which my husband also dared to intervene by saying that there had to be an alternative to the unwanted visit to an emergency room, the man said that the only place he would agree to be taken to was an apothecary eight blocks down the street. "Kill me there," smiled the man, with the blissful condescension I had noticed in him when we'd first met.

It was still early, but the sunset was already glowing the color of dried blood when we arrived at the apothecary. We had walked to the cadence of the man and his guitar cane. In the apothecary, tended by a Dominican teenager, I felt at peace among the shelves crammed with candles, herbs, plaster saints, colored ribbons, and bottles of homemade concoctions, a feeling that I attributed not to the magical or metaphysical pretensions of the business, but to the recognition of a cultural background that augured, if only for a few moments, a place in the world for me. A place in New York for me too.

After a while, the real owner of the apothecary finally came out and, after serving him a tea that smelled like a blend of oregano and something else, they took the man into a small back room. It was then that the Rastas decided that they'd reached the limit of their Samaritanism and left. They were leaving on good terms with their civic consciences; surely, they needed to reward themselves with a couple grams of lines for such a good deed. To them too, the man had said, "May God repay you with that thing your hearts wish for so bad." Who knew whether that was a blessing or not.

We waited a little over an hour, attentive to the sounds of household instruments, liquids simmering, and muffled moans. I did not see The Man with the Leg again. The owner came out of the back room and, without taking off his medical mask or his bloody apron, handed us a thick, gray bag and assured us that the man was fine, that he would wake up in a few hours in pain but could spend the night there and that he'd check on him tomorrow.

Dumbfounded, we took the bag without hesitation. "How much do we owe you?" my husband asked sheepishly. He was hoping that the supportive Rastas had left some money to cover their brilliant idea of healing the man. The owner pulled down his mask and said that these kinds of operations had no cost, this was a real apothecary, not one of those bogus little shops that don't have the slightest knowledge of supernatural forces.

"Well," he said with astonishing patience, "you can do me a favor and take the contents of this bag to the sanctuary. I'll show you where it is. I have an important offering to make, and this will work well; it's organic."

As darkness settled and the biting cold set in mercilessly, I made a calculated decision to remove my thick scarf and conceal the bag. Carefully wrapping it up, I tucked it close to my tits, hoping to avoid drawing any unwanted attention. Yet, even as I did so, a sense of unease gnawed at me. What was there to suspect? Our so-called "crime" was nothing more than a complex web of individual desires that had long since overwhelmed the fragile barriers of our impulses. The marks left from trying to induce ovulation had driven me to the brink of madness, leaving me feeling like a desperate Daisy or a beautiful Clarabelle, fighting against the current of my own desires.

We took the subway instead of walking to the sanctuary. We decided not to walk because of the dead weight of the bag—which I refused to give to my husband because of the cracked skin on his knuckles. The train was packed. It was the time of day when people were heading home, all sweaty and tired. Our dissatisfaction bonded us. Overall, it would be only a few miles to the sanctuary. However, just then a woman offered me her seat. "Cover your baby, sweetie," she advised. "There are a lot of sick people here."

And that's what I did: I cradled the bag wrapped in my scarf and took a deep breath, feeling the now discreet and sweetly fetid scent of the offering, and only then did I start to cry, slowly, while the train continued its fatal march through the cold bowels of New York.

ANTONIO DÍAZ OLIVA
(ADO)
TRANSLATED BY LISA DILLMAN

LUEGO DE NUESTRA EXPERIENCIA FORMATIVA
Y LUEGO DE LA DESAPARICIÓN DE JORGE,
CON RAQUEL DECIDIMOS CASARNOS.

RABBITS

AFTER OUR FORMATIVE EXPERIENCE, AND JORGE'S DISAP-pearance, Raquel and I decided to get married. Her mother was happy, she even cried, said we'd be happy, that it was the right decision, without a doubt; her father, on the other hand, was more reserved in his felicitations and, after a few minutes, went and shut himself in his room.

The old man was like that. Silent and restrained.

He'd lock himself up with his books, his maps, our journals. He spoke only rarely to his wife, and to Raquel even less. Of course, while it's true that Raquel's parents didn't talk to each other much back then, I didn't understand that there was something lurking beneath that silence. I was eighteen, newly returned from my formative experience, and struggled to grasp, in those early days as Raquel's husband, that the silence between her parents was the same one that enveloped the entire commune.

*

But this was no Bavaria Village, no Colonia Dignidad. Just a hippie commune. Chilean hippies, which are not the same as gringo hippies or European hippies. Still, to the military, we belonged to the same category as those German groups off somewhere in the south, which is why when they found us, in the '80s, after the commune had been up and running for nearly ten years, they made a deal. Why didn't they just take us all prisoner? Send us to the National Stadium or Dawson Island? I don't know. Sometimes I wonder that too. I look back at some of the photos, the ones of the founding members, with their long hair, dirty clothes, sandals, and backpacks—later they did get more formal—and I wonder.

And I truly don't know.

I was young, but not that young. Plus, my mother was one of the founders, though I don't remember much about her, now that I'm trying to reconstruct the story. My father I remember even less, since he was one of the first deserters.

*

The formative experience, yes, I'm getting to that.

*

At the age of seventeen, after a ceremony, all of the founders' children were sent out for a year of freedom. We had preparatory sessions. Spent more time than usual with our families. Were released from evening chores. And we were given two hours to write in our formative journals. What did we write? Anything. Anything that came into our heads; any act or event we felt was important to our human development. Until the day arrived.

Of course, there was no knowing what day that would be, since it was a surprise. There would be a knock on the door, one of the founders would take us to the wooden gate—usually Raquel's father, who was the closest thing the commune had to a leader—and say goodbye, and suddenly we'd be on the outside, in the elements. There we were. We walked down a road. It was this rocky trail, and it took nearly two and a half hours to get to a wooden hut where someone was awaiting us. We never found out who, though it was probably some soldier in civilian clothing, delegated by Pinochet, aka Pinocchio, to ensure that the community remained isolated. He'd be the one to take us to the city in a minivan that, I later learned, was the same as the kind used to take children to and from school. The drive brought us to a big house in the center of the city. And that's when our formative experience began. A year to do whatever we wanted. Enough money for the first few months.

And at the end of the year, a decision: either we went back to the commune, or we left it forever.

*

There were a few signs. Like, shortly before our formative experience, my mother died. Or like, the first rabbits began to appear, though in the beginning we didn't take much notice.

When my mother died, I was sent to live with Raquel and her parents. I was sixteen, so this was a year before my formative experience. One thing I never understood was why they wouldn't let me see her before she died, why I wasn't allowed to say *ciao, vieja, I'll miss you, thanks for everything*; why they wouldn't let me close her eyes myself, with my own hands. Raquel's father denied me that, just as, years later, he forbade Raquel from seeing her mother's body. Said it was part of our education.

That we'd be better for it.

Whole beings, physically and spiritually.

I remember that at the ceremony—it was the same funeral ceremony when anyone from the commune died— my mother had already been buried, and they gathered us all to pray. Then the founders reminisced about the newly departed. And after that we held hands and had a moment of silence. I didn't feel the urge to cry. I think, for the first time, what I felt was rage. Rage at not knowing who controlled my life. Raquel's father concluded the ceremony. That morning—a Sunday, I believe—Raquel came up to me, took my hand, and told me we were going to live together. I gave her a smile, but it was hollow. I kissed her. We were already boyfriend and girlfriend by that time. Founders' kids mixed from a young age in our commune. And the founders liked that, of course; it was the only way to keep multiplying, since we had no contact with the outside world.

*

I had no trouble adapting to Raquel's family. In part because, when my mother died, I became a silent creature, unlike the person I am today. I had no self-awareness, and no awareness of what was going on around me. I went to the commune school in the morning and to the fields to work my shift in the afternoon; I went to all of the mandatory activities for founders' kids. But I wasn't really present. I adapted to Raquel's house because it was functional and silent; and, in the end, functional people, the ones who still have no regrets, were the ones who never opened their mouths. I was functional back then too. I believed in the commune and did exactly what was asked of me, to the letter. But my mother's death split my life in two: a happy and obedient past and an uncertain present, flat and dull as the commune activities. As the speeches the founders made us memorize; indeed, as the legacy we would supposedly inherit.

*

Raquel was washing the dishes and I was drying. It was night; we'd already finished dinner. There was this game we used to play, telling the difference between what we remembered and what we thought we remembered from our childhood. Raquel was talking about this image she had of her father, back when he'd been a singer in a band. But actually, she said, rinsing the wooden cutlery, what I truly remember is a song. What song, I asked? I wanted to know if she really did remember the song, or if it was a memory of someone telling her about the song. She didn't reply. There were still dishes with little chunks of polenta and spinach on them. I asked again. What song, Raq? She didn't reply. Look, she said. And pointed out the window. I looked. Through the glass I saw two red dots and then, elsewhere on the patio, two more red dots. And then two more. And two more. And on and on until I began to feel afraid. Raquel dropped the dishtowel and the knife she was washing and stood still a few seconds. I remember that the sounds of her father working filtered up through the stairwell that night; you could hear the sound of the typewriter, one of the few items every family in the commune was allowed. Raquel was still frozen. Raquel? I asked. She didn't reply. Raquel? I repeated, louder. She walked out the kitchen door. I followed. We tried to find the red dots again, but you couldn't see a thing. The darkness out on the patio, which had a wooden swing set nobody used anymore and a stone-lined trench for compost, was just a dense, black backdrop. As with every house in the commune, the only source of light came from a wooden streetlamp with a candle. And in its glow, there appeared the first of many rabbits we'd see over the years to come. Quivering, its fur all dirty. It looked at us and then disappeared. It was big.

That night Raquel went down to her father's study and told him. She was trembling. I stayed upstairs in the kitchen, finishing the dishes. Earlier that night, before the rabbits, Raquel's mother had said she felt ill and retired early. Her father had a quick dinner with us, excused himself, and then went down to his study. I used to think he was working on his memoir. Or a manifesto. Now I know none of that was true. That night I heard Raquel scream. I didn't do anything, just kept washing dishes. Her father told her off for interrupting him. There was more and more screaming, but I tried to think about something else. And despite the inner voice telling me to go down there to defend Raquel, I also had to follow the rules of the commune. I couldn't forget that I was part of a human collective. And that we had to respect what bound us together. I finished washing the cutlery, went up to the bedroom, lay down, closed my eyes, and pretended to sleep.

The following morning, the patio was wrecked. And it wasn't just ours; the rest of the commune had been damaged too. Some houses had been gnawed at the edges; there were clear scratches and tooth marks. Initially, some people doubted that it had actually been rabbits. But then, there was also that noise at night. It was hard to sleep with that noise. I still remember it: soft whimpering, shrieking, rabbits darting along the perimeter of the house like rats. Plus there was their poop: little black pellets that mushroomed on the patio. And this became another chore for the kids on the commune. We had to pick it up and throw it into the stone trench.

At one point, people thought it might be some other animal: the Chupacabra, somebody said. Or wild pumas. Or rabid pudus. People even thought the invasion might be a plot to destabilize the commune. That a group of frontists and communists wanted to get rid of us. Or even the military, who were now retreating. After all, on the inside, few people knew what was going on in Chile: that it was 1988, that the left was reconfiguring, the military about to leave power. Then one day Raquel's father walked into the house. In one hand he held a rifle, and in the other, one of the rabbits—by the ears. It was trembling. He put it on a wooden cutting board. The thing looked halfdead. Raquel's father took a rolling pin out of a drawer. He looked at me and raised his arm. Gave it a quick blow behind the ears.

*

My formative experience was like therapy. It was only once I left the commune that I felt free. It happened the day that Raquel, Jorge—the son of some other founders, also out on his experience—and I were put in a minivan and taken to the city. I remember the military dude who was driving (and who we didn't know was military; he had gray hair and a reedy voice). Jorge kept asking him questions. The guy was laughing and teasing him. But Jorge wouldn't stop asking questions. The guy said if he kept on like that he'd take him back to the damn hippies. Then Jorge said he couldn't because he had to spend a year in the city. He said, We choose whether to go back or stay on the outside. And the dude laughed. Outside, he said. Y'sure you really wanna be outside?

Me and Raquel were in the back seat, holding hands. I had a rabbit's foot in my pocket for good luck. I'd made it myself, the week before, while Raquel's parents were at the amphitheater for one of the many weekly meetings. Raquel had been tired and gone to bed early. Maybe she was nervous.

We sensed that it was going to happen that week. We'd heard a lot about the formative experience, but it was impossible to predict. Anyway, something told me we'd be on the outside that week. Unable to sleep, that night I steeled myself and went down to the living room. I walked in circles for a while. Then, without thinking about it too much, I went into Raquel's father's study. I knew where to find it, in a drawer with linen cloths, towels, and pumice stones. I took it and went out onto the patio.

You could hear this grunting. I saw a couple red dots. I walked in the dark. Hopped the fence. The minute I heard rustling I took aim. Three shots: the first one almost brought me down with the recoil; the other two I withstood a little better. The gun felt heavy in my hand. I looked at it closely then: the wooden butt, moonlight reflected in its varnish; the trigger cold and hard as a block of ice that burned to the touch. It was hefty. I leaned the rifle against the patio fence. I can still recall the image of a skull exploding into pieces, some so small they were lost in the grass. It was nighttime and I relished this small catharsis. My vieja was dead, and I was all alone in the world, but something had changed. I felt the urge to go to the amphitheater and kill all the founders, escape the commune, cross the Andes. Leave this country that wasn't my country because I'd spent my life confined to a land of familiar faces. Too familiar.

I thought of Raquel.

I gathered up all the pieces of skull I could find in the dark. Next I pulled out a knife, severed one of the rabbit's back feet, wrapped it in a cloth, and stuck it in my left pocket. And then I took the decapitated body, went to the stone trench, and tossed it in with the rest of the rabbits.

*

Part of the formative experience involved keeping a journal in which we recorded thoughts, ideas, drawings, whatever went through our heads. At the end of the year, if we returned, we had to hand it in to be reviewed. Raquel's father was the one in charge of this.

Anyway, as I said, it was Jorge, Raquel, and me. But what became of Jorge? And who was he? Like the rest of us, he had no last name. Jorge was Jorge, just Jorge, and I think of him now as an extrovert; he was rarely silent and his parents were the volatile sort at the commune—people who never fully committed to the utopian ideal but would still rather be there than on the outside, with the military. It was odd. They didn't attend the meetings at the amphitheater and instead made the bread and cheese, milked the cows. Or they tended the animals. But the weird thing is that Jorge was the opposite: he went to all of the activities gladly, always had a positive attitude, and made an effort. He was the perfect son, with his snaggletooth smile and bushy eyebrows. That's why Raquel's father was so fond of him, much more so than he was of me. Jorge was the ideal accomplice; at first, he had no idea what was truly going on at the commune, and then later, when he accidentally found out, he kept quiet about it.

Anyway, that afternoon we got to the city, and then Raquel and I spent at least two months locked in our room. I won't deny it, we had some beautiful times, not learning a thing about the city, but fucking every morning and afternoon like the rabbits that were multiplying back on the commune that year. Because someone wanted them to multiply. But at the time we knew nothing about any of that. There was this handbook at the house with instructions and advice on how to make sense of society during our time there. How and what to buy at the supermarket. Curfew. Who Pinochet was and who Allende had been. I mean, we had Chilean history classes at the commune, of course, but they didn't want to leave anything to chance. The year we spent in the city would either reinforce or undermine our loyalty. That was the test.

Jorge shut himself up in his room too. Mostly, he wrote in his journal. Wrote and, from time to time, emerged to eat with us. I'd ask him questions and he'd respond with what we'd learned in our classes about inner lives, temperaments, and so on. But I started to notice he had less energy. I watched him languish over the months. I, on the other hand, felt renewed, as if I'd stolen Jorge's enthusiasm.

And then one day, when it was his turn to do the shopping, Raquel and I went into his room and read his journal. At first we found nothing. Just stuff about the city, the flavor of chocolate, the woman who kept everything in order, the first time he watched TV. But then Raquel came across a different kind of entry. Third person. It was like a short story. The tale of a commune boy who hid under the amphitheater stage. He was made of wood. Tree Boy, Jorge wrote: Tree Boy does this, Tree Boy does that. It was like a children's story, kind of dark. Naïve in tone. Pages and pages of what happened to Tree Boy. Nothing particularly interesting, until one day Tree Boy went and hid under the amphitheater stage again and the founders turned up. They started talking about a special meeting. About the deserter. About *cleansing* the community. And then the deserter, it seems, was brought out onto the stage. They had him tied up. Gagged. From below, Tree Boy listened closely. Frightened by the blows, at first, and then shocked to hear a song accompanied by guitar and more shouting and a wail that began just as the song ended and grew louder and louder until finally it became a death lament.

*

Jorge disappeared a month before we returned to the commune. Raquel and I knew he wouldn't go back. But it was still odd. We found his clothes, his belongings, nearly all of his journals. We reread them. He'd stopped writing regular entries a while ago. Now all he did was rehash the story about the boy in the amphitheater overhearing those sounds. What changed was the tone, the tale growing ever darker and less childlike. I regret it now, but on the last day of our formative experience I threw away his journals.

We returned to the commune, Raquel and I. Didn't even discuss the possibility of remaining in the city. We'd been happy on the outside, sure, but only because our time there had an expiration date. If our experience reinforced anything, it was that we loved each other. And that on the inside, in the commune, we had food, shelter, and a spiritual refuge. The three elements every human being needs.

On our return they held an oathtaking ceremony, and we told Raquel's parents and the other founders about Jorge. We got married. Two ceremonies in two weeks. The oathtaking and our wedding. Both of us dressed in white, Raquel in leather sandals, me in brown shoes. I thought a lot about my mother that day. I don't know whether she'd have liked me getting married so young. But I felt indebted to Raquel.

I'm not too clear on when Raquel's parents started fighting. Maybe we were the cause of it; our wedding, I mean. Or maybe it started earlier, when Raquel's mother left the commune, already very sick. It was obvious that even if they'd called every one of the commune doctors and used all the stockpiled homeopathic medicine, she still would have needed to go to the medical center.

After that, Raquel's mother started spending the mornings in bed. She no longer worked. It didn't matter. She was a founder, one of the original group. And she didn't have to be productive in the fields like me, like Raquel and everybody else. Only when someone was very sick could they leave the commune. Only then was that person transported to a medical center where we had a deal—one of those deals that we kids never knew about. A few years earlier, I'd actually been taken to that same medical center when my appendix burst. I think I was fourteen, and my mother was still alive at the time. The pain was so intense I was hallucinating and, honestly, I don't remember much about leaving the commune. I'd fainted in the fields while picking carrots. I saw lights and had a dream where, for some reason, I had a job cleaning swimming pools, though I didn't know what a swimming pool was because I'd never seen one. Or at least that's what I thought, until my mother told me that, when I was born, a few years before joining the commune, the first thing she and my father did was throw me into the water, so I'd learn to swim.

When I woke up in the medical center, I was wearing a white robe. I thought I'd died but then my mother came over with one of the nurses. I saw lights and two silhouettes. There was still dirt under my fingernails. My head hurt. Then I saw that her hair had turned white, and I realized how much of that white had appeared over those few days; my mother had grown old in the time I was hospitalized. She said hello. Told me everything was going to be okay. Said that in a few days I'd be released. She smiled. I felt a cold cloth on my forehead. It was one of the last times I saw her happy. Her eyes were black and her eyebrows, which had also turned white, were knit so close they almost joined.

That night and the next I was cared for by a nurse who kept a rabbit's foot in the pocket of her uniform, a nurse who, I noticed through the hall door, would take it out and rub it before going into the operating room. I don't know why, but I made an effort not to forget that image. She seemed to project some kind of healing energy by rubbing it in her hands. Since then, I've always felt that a rabbit's foot meant something. And I still carry one with me.

*

I don't believe this, but people say that the same nurse was there when Raquel's mother ran away. I wonder if she did it because she had cancer and knew she was going to die. Or if it was because she'd always wanted to escape the commune. In subsequent years, I only heard it brought up two or three times. Raquel kept quiet about it, and not much information circulated in the commune. We knew it was done quickly; one night when she was hospitalized, Raquel's mother disconnected the tubes she was hooked up to and escaped down the hall. Outside, at the far end of the parking lot, a man was waiting for her in a van, the engine running. But not any old van—the same minivan that had driven us to our formative experience. Then she died. We don't know where, in what bed, beside whom. That still pains Raquel. And me. Which is why I've taken it upon myself to respond to everyone who wants to know about the commune. Still, like I told you, in this case there is no pure-white truth. Even now, telling you all this, I have to massage a few details. Adjust them. Otherwise all that's left are isolated events. As isolated as we were, up in the mountains.

*

Not long after that, I noticed Raquel was feeling down on herself. I think it was the fights with her father, or maybe the fact that we were trying to have a kid and it wasn't working, I don't know. Raquel was in that angry phase, full of hatred for the founders. Sooner or later it happened to everyone. We learned about it in class: at some point in our spiritual development, we'd experience periods of hatred and questioning. The angry phase. Raquel was in that phase. She threw it all in her father's face: we weren't allowed to experience the world; we were trapped; they were a bunch of old fogeys willing to sacrifice anything, even their families, to avoid confronting what was happening on the outside and, especially, to avoid confronting themselves.

Since I no longer had a mother, and my father was one of the early deserters, I never went through that phase. I always kept the hatred in. Maybe now I'm letting it out. Bit by bit.

What the fuck are we doing here, Raquel once asked her father. And he grabbed her by the hand, hard, and told her to calm down, said he couldn't deal with a hysterical daughter when he was taking care of more important things, like saving the commune. This is all we've got, her father said. If we lose this, we lose ourselves.

The following morning, I found Raquel crying in the bathroom and said, We're out of here. She looked at me uncomprehendingly. I wiped her tears. Get your stuff together. We're out of here, I repeated. Raquel slowly shook her head. No, she said. Then she asked if I was sure, if something awful might not happen to us on the outside, now that the country seemed to be changing. I grabbed both of her hands hard, so it hurt, so she would feel that I loved her, and said that from then on she had to listen to me.

I'm going to take care of you, I said.

We walked for twelve hours. Circled our way down the mountain until we got to the highway. To soothe her, I asked Raquel to tell me about her father's song, the one from when he was the singer in a band. She recounted her memories. Over and over. And all the effort led her to recall a line from the song: "Where do they all come from?"

It was a long walk. The hut was no longer on the path. Nor was that dude, the one with gray hair and a reedy voice who was probably military; now there was nobody. It seemed like something had changed. Raquel was trembling and I told her to calm down—not shouting, but I did give her a serious look. I love you, I said. She saw that I'd protect her and took my hand.

*

Three years after our formative year, the city was almost the same, though maybe not as many military. We spent a few days on the streets. Then we found a place to sleep and got jobs, doing anything, whatever would give us food and shelter, and only then, once we had both of those things, did Raquel calm down. Still, I kept giving her orders and telling her I loved her. Every time I spoke to her, I'd raise my voice and grab her hands hard, like her father.

We slept at a hostel in the center of town, next to the bus station. We had something resembling a life, though from time to time, here and there, visions appeared, images of the commune, the founders, Raquel's mother's escape and all that. We kept working, trying to go unnoticed, but it wasn't easy. We wanted to forget and to be forgotten. To reinvent ourselves. One day we went to the registry office. Said we needed IDs to work. Took a number. Stood in line. Waited. Saw people going up to a window. And then it was our turn. We said we had no papers. They were stolen, we said. A cop came over to ask for our details. They asked us about the robbery, about ourselves, and then about the commune. We told the truth. A distorted truth, like what I'm giving you. The commune, yes, we said. No, we don't know where our parents are. Yes, years ago we had our formative experience in the city. No, we didn't know anything about that. We spent the afternoon in a big, cold room. There was a bunk attached to the wall. The civil registry closed and they turned on some lights. Dim lights. They brought us a television and on screen was a presenter beside a man in a black hood. The one in the black hood was playing a trumpet. The presenter shouted and perspired. They called him Don Francisco. Raquel calmed down. So did I. We watched the same channel all afternoon. It never occurred to us to ask what we were doing there, when they were going to let us go, until they told us it was time for dinner and Raquel's father appeared. He seemed the same as ever.

Silent and restrained.

The cops left. Left us alone. The room now seemed enormous. Inescapable. Raquel's father was holding two red plastic trays. On each one was a plate with fried potatoes, lettuce, tomato, and a soft pinkish piece of meat, which he forced us to eat.

Children, he said. Dinner.

And pointed to the steamed rabbit.

*

I won't bore you with the rest. The truth is that not much happened until people got all cultish about it. All those dipshits who started investigating what happened in the late '70s and discovered the commune and the deal they had with the military. Journalists, academics, politicians, writers. They can all go fuck themselves. As if we didn't have enough trauma and pointless regret already, as if the national memory weren't soiled enough already. Why pour salt on a wound that's begun to heal? I only tell the whole story to people like you, people with power.

The last time I saw Raquel's father was at the hearings. That same week somebody burned down the commune's amphitheater. And that's when it was discovered that people were tortured there and their bodies ended up in the stone trench, along with the rabbits. Those rabbits, along with democracy, were what put an end to the commune, a plague brought on by Raquel's father and the military themselves.

That week we appeared on television. The trials were held. And since I wasn't the child of any of the living founders, they let me go free. All I had to do was testify. But Raquel.

I don't know what happened to her.

All I know is that in one of the hearings she called me a traitor.

Two days later I got my identity card. And changed my name. Almost left the country.

But I chose to stay.

Now I do what I dreamed of that night in the hospital, when I hallucinated and saw my mother for the last time. I have these blue overalls that I wear every day. It's been years now. I get on buses going to Las Condes, to Vitacura, to Lo Curro. Not that far from the commune. Once I actually cleaned the pool at a house I recognized. I was sure I'd seen it the first day of our formative experience, when we were in the minivan, Raquel and I holding hands. Sweaty hands. Nervous. Happy. Jorge and the military dude in the front seat.

Sometimes when nobody's around, I get in the pools. Or talk to the cleaning ladies. Some of them actually invite me in for lunch and even let me use the computer. Yesterday, for instance, I saw that Raquel's father has two Wikipedia entries. I've actually been obsessed with Wikipedia for some time now. I edit everything related to the past that I want to control. That's why I rewrote a few of the entries; why in one of them the old man appears as the Chilean Charles Manson, leader of the mountain commune; and in the other as the vocalist of the High Alpacas, a '60s rock band who played at Piedra Roja and is now only remembered for "Where Do They All Come From?" a cover of the Beatles' "Eleanor Rigby." That's the song Raquel remembered, or thought she did, the first night of the rabbit plague. And the one I hum when I clean pools, when I'm trying to get to sleep, when I think we didn't really have it so bad. On the inside we had food, shelter, and a spiritual refuge. The three elements every human being needs.

LAZARUS

CLAUDIA HERNÁNDEZ

TRANSLATED BY JULIA SANCHES
AND JOHANNA WARREN

THE VULTURE

DE VEZ EN CUANDO, A LÁZARO SE LE SALÍA EL INSTINTO.

From time to time, instinct got the better of Lazarus. This happened mostly at funerals, where we always had to keep him away from the body because otherwise he would get too close and say aloud that he wanted to eat it, that it stirred his appetite. Then we would take him to the nearest restaurant to have a drink and a bite to eat.

He would order raw meat as a reminder of "the tasty morsel I just left in the coffin." We would pretend it was the funniest joke we had ever heard, even though we knew he was being serious. Underneath his suit and his smile, Lazarus was a vulture like any other. He didn't try to hide it. He didn't trim his talons or fold his wings, except when he traveled by bus, out of consideration for the other passengers. But the second he was outside he would unfurl them again and, if he was in a particularly good mood, take flight, soaring over the city and painting our granite sky with his wings.

Whether in flight or on land, he was always a conversation piece. People would smile and say hello, not because he was a vulture, but because he was charming, good-natured. He went around the city doling out polite remarks and sparking conversation at every corner. Since he always had something to say, he was never excluded for being a vulture; or for having feathers embedded in his skin and a giant beak instead of a mouth; or for being as tall as a man, which made him very large for a vulture. He behaved like a man. He went out early to buy the afternoon paper. He was a model citizen, even though his papers weren't in order and he never made any effort to obtain them.

Everyone was fond of him—strangers on the street, neighbors, even me, despite the fact that I had to put up with his silence in the apartment above mine—because he was fun to be around. He told the best jokes. They'd make you laugh even if you had vinegar pumping through your veins. You could forgive him anything for the sake of his company. His penchant for raw meat when we went out for dinner, his arrogance when he talked about how wonderful it felt to fly without being trapped in an airplane, the dusty smell of his feathers, even his habit of exiting through the window instead of the door like the rest of us. All these things were excusable. I even forgave him for snatching my wife's dog from the terrace one day when he was especially hungry (we mustn't deny food to our neighbors) and accidently scratching my daughter's arms with his talons on another day, when he grabbed her during a game. What I couldn't forgive was how eagerly he lapped up her blood with his own tongue.

My wife, oblivious to bad intentions, told him not to feel bad, that our daughter was young and hardy, the cut would heal in no time. She even kissed his cheek in gratitude as he went on licking the wound, smiling and tickling our daughter. She laughed like everyone else, convinced he was playing. It was as if they'd forgotten that no one who is playing looks as ravenously as he did at my daughter.

Lazarus wanted to eat her, just like the dog he'd eaten and the corpses he wished to eat at funerals, just like the raw meat he ate at restaurants and the thousands of animals he must have eaten wherever he came from. I knew it. I was on to him. Noticing this, he came over to apologize, to say he still had trouble controlling certain impulses and that I mustn't think he wished my daughter any harm. I honestly wanted to believe him. But at night, as I lay dreaming, I saw him fly off clutching my wife's dead dog in his beak, my son and daughter in his talons. He devoured them with relish and then, amid a vast kettle of vultures, descended upon the other residents of the city.

Seeing how nervous I looked in the days that followed, he started inviting me out so we could put the past behind us. I turned him down most of the time. Finally, I said yes and took him hunting with me, telling no one and giving him no time to tell anyone about where he was going. He was delighted and, as we made our way to the hunting grounds, harped on and on about all the prized catches he would be bringing home thanks to his skilled flying, keen eyesight, and talons. Every time he said this, his eyes gleamed with desire.

Once we were in the country, he flew up high and drew circles in the sky while I pretended to look for hares. Every so often, Lazarus would swoop down with an enormous catch skewered in his claws. He would drop the dead animal at my feet, look at me with malice, and boast that the next one would be even bigger. I smiled.

After seven kills, he flew up high and began drawing circles in the patch of sky right above me. The time had come. Before he had a chance to lunge at me, I shot him. As he swirled proudly in the air, I shot him. As he fell, wounded, I shot him. I shot him again when he hit the ground. Even after he was dead, I shot him. Then I went home, where no one remarked on my absence because I came back at the same time as I do every day.

Whenever anyone mentioned how he didn't come by anymore or they hadn't seen him out flying in a while, I suggested that maybe he had left, just like that, with no warning, the same as he had arrived. Hadn't they noticed he'd never gotten his papers? I even suggested that maybe he had never been, had never existed, that his name wasn't Lazarus, that he was merely a collective dream. People stopped worrying and soon forgot all about him, and I decided to do the same. So, when the landlord came by one afternoon to clear out his belongings, I lamented his sudden disappearance, like everyone else, and helped pack all his things into boxes. I made sure there was no trace of him left, not even a suit, and helped clean up the space in preparation for the eventual arrival of our new neighbor.

THE
HOUSE OF
COMPASSION

CAMILA SOSA VILLADA
TRANSLATED BY KIT MAUDE

ES   LA   PAMPA   CORDOBESA.   AL   SUR.

I

THE CÓRDOBA PAMPAS. TO THE SOUTH.

The vista is flat and depressing. The horizon; the roads; the deathly smell of pesticides sprayed over the fields; the fathomlessly melancholy, elongated sky, which never gets quite blue enough. The trucks cruelly speeding by. And also, impossible to ignore, the proximity of the city not so many miles away.

But right now, we're only concerned with the pampas. A gas station, the wind blowing resolutely unchecked, and a few parked cars. Some are filling their gas tanks, others are getting something to eat, some just need to use the bathroom. You won't find many clean bathrooms around here.

A small car, a red Ford Ka carrying a small family—mom, dad, and a girl—slows down.

"I told you to go before we left," the mother scolds the child, furious because now she's going to have to set foot in a bathroom that, as we've already established, is bound to be filthy.

"Yes, Ma, if you've said it once, you've said it a hundred times. Shouting about it won't help."

The mother has slammed the door shut and is heading for the door with an L for Ladies.

"Then you can go in on your own. I'll be out here, smoking."

The girl rushes inside and opens a stall barely big enough to fit a toilet. She pees desperately.

"Don't touch the toilet, don't touch the bowl for goodness' sake!" the mother calls from outside.

A shiver of relief runs through her. Oh, what a lovely feeling! Someone flushes in the next stall over. It's a good thing she's still holding in that fart. What if someone heard? A sweet perfume floats over from the other side of the tiled wall.

She dries herself from front to back with a piece of toilet paper the way her mom showed her and goes straight out to wash her hands. The woman is standing with her back to her. She's wearing high-heeled boots and a very short miniskirt and has skinny, toned legs. She's very tall. And so skinny! The girl likes her makeup, the kind you see in science fiction movies, colors glittering all over. It sparkles more when she shakes out her hair.

"Would you like to wash your hands?"

The girl nods shyly, terrified. She's not tall enough to reach the faucet. The woman's voice is metallic, nasal, the voice you'd expect from a travesti. *Is she...? Maybe she... Oh... I'll die if I've met a real travesti. Die, die, die, wait until the girls at school hear about this. If Mom comes in now, I'll die. She's got lipstick on her teeth. Should I tell her? No, don't say anything. She'll see when she checks herself in the mirror.*

"Would you like some soap?"

The girl nods again and cups her hands underneath the dispenser, which is also out of her reach.

The travesti's hand is large and hairy, like a dog's paw.

"What's your name?"

"Flor," she answers as she continues to smear on her lipstick. As though she didn't have plenty on already. She rubs her stained teeth with her finger.

"I'm Magda."

"That's a nice name. What are you doing here?"

"We're going to my grandmother's wake in Córdoba. We're coming back tomorrow night. My mom's angry."

"Because she has to go to Córdoba?"

"No, she didn't want to come by car because of the accidents."

The travesti turns off the faucet, grabs some paper towels, and hands them to her to dry her hands.

"Want to know my full name?"

The girl nods again.

"My name is Flor de Ceibo Argañaraz."

And as though trying to change the subject after her revelation, she adds:

"You have beautiful eyes. I love their color. I recognize the gleam I had when I was your age."

Time appears to have stopped. They can't hear the trucks, or the cars dopplering by. It's as though the whole of the pampas has disappeared.

"You know where that gleam comes from?"

The girl shakes her head and fixes a pair of eyes that look fit to burst on the woman.

"Fear of grown-ups. You know? Don't you think grown-ups are scary?"

"Oh."

"Aren't you ever scared of grown-ups?"

"Yes, sometimes. But I also feel sorry for them."

"Sorry?"

"Yes, I feel bad for them. My friends and I are always saying how we feel bad for our parents."

She's a feisty little one. Intelligent and feisty.

"You're right to be scared of grown-ups. I used to be like you; my eyes gleamed."

"Can I ask you a question without you getting upset?"

"Of course, honey, nothing upsets me."

"Are you a travesti?"

"Yes, and one of the most authentic ones you're likely to find around here. One hundred percent travesti."

"When I tell the girls at school, they won't believe it..."

Magda's mother's knuckles rap on the metal door. She's just finished her cigarette and remembered that she has a daughter.

"Come on, Magda! What are you up to in there? Hurry up, your father's waiting for us in the car."

"Go. And remember: the ceibo is our national flower. Maybe you'll think of me some day."

The moment she's out, her mother locks her in a vice-like grip and marches her back to the car.

"Magda, were you talking to someone?"

"No, I was singing. What's a national flower? Like the queen of flowers? Which is Argentina's national flower?"

"How should I know? Where is this coming from?"

The father has bought sodas and chips at the store. The wind is corrosive and persistent enough to make you suicidal. The girl in the back seat is already drinking her Coke.

"Put on your seatbelt."

The mother swallows her chips and looks out at the road stretching ahead of her. The father starts the car and, just as it's moving off, a big dog steps out in front of it and turns to look at them. Magda screams:

"Stop, Daddy! You're going to run it over!"

"You see? I told you, this road is dangerous."

The dog doesn't move until the girl holds a chip out the window. It comes over and leaps up onto the door. The mother screeches in fright. The animal takes the chip delicately from Magda's hand.

"Come on, let's go before the dog gets in with us!"

The car pulls out and disappears down the road.

II

Now we see Flor de Ceibo coming out of the bathroom. She's stumbling from side to side. Maybe the girl didn't notice how drunk she was, or maybe she just ignored it. There goes this splendid example of womanhood in her silver lurex miniskirt, short enough for her and her alone, and her weathered boots with the heel bent back but still roadworthy. They even have a kind of refinement. Underneath the jean jacket she altered and cut the tassels off herself, she's wearing a top that barely covers her hormone-induced breasts. "Men don't see these things. They don't know how to appreciate them.

You could have a peacock sticking out your ass singing in Mandarin and they'd barely notice. You dress for yourself, that's how it is, that's why you're a travesti," an old travesti said to her once in La Piaf, a gay dive that was both her school and her paradise.

Flor de Ceibo has had a long night. She saw to six johns. The sun hits her face. She looks in her handbag for her sunglasses but can't find them. There's not a shadow to be found in the pampas. "You need to settle down. Go to Rosario. There, the guys go nuts over queens. Out here on the road, if you're not killed by a farmer, you'll be hit by a car," the same travesti said to her on another occasion. "There, when you stick out your ass it never touches the ground. These guys fuck you in mid-air. Listen to me. One weekend a month. You'll come back fucked by a bunch of bull chongos and rolling in money. Then you can give it all to that idiot you live with."

Flor de Ceibo considers her friend's advice. Things have been pretty ugly around here recently. Johns don't want to pay what she's asking, and she has to work more to make the same money she used to from just two or three guys. They too are afraid of hitting an animal crossing the road and ending up a shrine surrounded by empty bottles and plastic flowers. It's time to make a move, try her luck in Rosario. Flor's grown tired of this fucked-up pampas highway routine.

But today that routine has a twist. In addition to meeting that girl—oh, what was her name, María, Marta, Mar...Magda, that was it, from the Bible—something else is going to happen.

A group of nuns is walking toward her on the other side of the road. They're from the Order of the Sisters of Compassion. They're amusing themselves, clinging on to their habits, which billow out and threaten to fly off when a car passes by. Flor de Ceibo stares at them, fascinated by how the light glints off their hoods and by their laughter at what the wind is doing beneath their rebellious skirts. Their legs are quite hairy, she notices at a gust of wind. Of course, nuns don't shave. They're looking back at her too. They bless her, smiling. One of them raises her hand in farewell. She's a young nun, maybe about fifty. She has a smile as wide as the pampas horizon, tooth after tooth stretching on forever. Flor de Ceibo smiles back, a little self-conscious about her missing premolar, and she thinks she sees a thick strand of drool dripping down the side of the nun's smiling face. A nun with false teeth? She doesn't trust them, no reason to deny it. But right now, she's fixated on the smile. What do they have underneath their habits, in addition to hairy legs? Flor pictures gigantic bloomers and iron chastity belts.

She turns several times to keep her eyes on the nuns. The nun who waved at her turns too. Now they're running. "I think she likes me," Flor de Ceibo says to the other Flor de Ceibo inside, who she's been talking to for years. There aren't many other people with whom she can have such sincere, entertaining conversations.

She turns down a dirt track that circumnavigates a football pitch, walks on about 150 feet and she's home. She opens the door and the metal scrapes against the concrete. The house groans. But it's a pretty house; flowers grow in the beds she waters every morning when she gets back from work. Snapdragons, begonias, hibiscus, busy lizzies, pansies, and geraniums. The façade is painted a very pale yellow, and from the outside you can see the thick curtains she cut and sewed herself. An autumnal motif with neatly stitched hems and ruffles. The entrance is a cement path with a stone surface she painted in every color that came to her in cast-off cans of paint. The only note out of place is the stone box containing the electricity meter where someone has spraypainted CHRIST IS CUMING in black. She should cover it up with something colorful, but right now she doesn't have the money to rid herself of the apocalyptic warning.

She puts her handbag down on the table, takes off her boots, and kicks them into a corner. Then she goes back out and picks up the hose already connected to a spigot at the entrance and waters the plants, humming a tune. Once the earth has turned a milky coffee color, she turns off the spigot and winds up the hose.

Now she heads into the bedroom. She pulls back the curtain, which she stitched herself as well, and the first thing she sees is a prone man. Her uncle has made himself at home, watching television as if he owned the place, lost in his cartoons. On the nightstand is a mug of coffee and the sheets are covered in crumbs, meaning that once again he's ignored her instructions to eat in the kitchen. She takes off her clothes and lets them fall to her feet. Her uncle doesn't look at her; his only reaction is to alter his breathing a little. He's about sixty, with a thin, pointy chest like the prow of a boat.

"Fucking hell. I forgot to take off my makeup."

She gets up with a sigh and goes to the bathroom to smother her face in cold cream. When she gets back, she looks miraculously younger. We have no way of knowing whether she knows that the makeup ages her. Maybe no one's ever told her, but like this, with her face bare, she definitely looks a lot younger. Now the uncle acknowledges her presence. He licks a finger and shoves it between her buttocks. She swats him away like an annoying fly.

"Stop it. Leave me alone."

"Huh...we'll see," says the old man before turning back to his cartoons.

Sometimes it's as though the heat takes a break and then the uncle's sweat dries on his skin and he gets cold. He reaches for her again. She pushes him away irritably and, naked as the day she was born, goes out to the garden to lie on a lounge chair.

The uncle, alone in the bedroom, travels back in time. He sees his nephew come in through the front door. A timid kid goat, already lost in the world, small bones and straight, jet-black hair. They dropped him off the same day that his sister died. He barely spoke. No more than yes, no, and uh-uh.

It was easy. He'd get back home from driving the taxi he had back then and sit him on his lap so they could watch cartoons together. He arranged his nephew's body as best suited him. He started stroking his knees, almost by accident, carelessly, until the boy's muscles relaxed, and one afternoon he leaned back against his chest. The boy's neck was very close to his mouth, and so he started to kiss his ears, like it was a joke. He saw goosebumps form all over the boy's skin. He kissed him on the mouth, his tongue probing as if looking for a wellspring, until it found one. After that he made him wash his shit-stained underwear and hit him every time he felt that life was unfair. It was a long, languorous crime, committed patiently.

Did that boy have bright eyes like Flor de Ceibo said a moment ago to the girl in the gas station bathroom? In the images bouncing around the uncle's head, you can't see very well, so we'll never know. But you must always believe people like her, even when they're not telling the truth.

One day, the nephew decided to paint his nails a pearly white and his skin began to smell of Hinds cream and Impulse deodorant. His uncle invited him to sleep with him. In the warm embrace of field-toughened arms, the pubescent flower slept with one eye open every night until his fears faded. He allowed his uncle in, and the man shoved deep enough to reach his belly button. Flor de Ceibo fell in love and considered the incestuous relationship a romance, with all the associated jealousy and petty squabbling. When money grew tight, she went out onto the street to make a living; at the end of the day, it was a worthy profession. She headed out to the road where she'd seen other travestis ply their trade and stuck with them. By the end of the first night, the same blood beat in her too. She was making her own money and could treat herself to things her uncle never gave her, like white coffee with medialuna croissants in the morning and Coca-Cola every day. She took a bus into the city, bought herself some clothes, and before long she was surrounded by guys desperate to make love to her in cheap but convenient motels. Her uncle grew lazy and sold the taxi. His belly grew and his teeth fell out. His frame became frail and his blond Cordóba-gringo hair turned dry and yellow. Flor was no longer willing to see to his needs in bed and she began to choke on the stench of poverty. She divorced him in secret. Around then she began to come to the realization, thanks to her friends on the road, that her uncle had used her for years. She cursed him in her own language, inside, with feeling. She stayed with him, but she made him pay for the shit he put her through with her heartfelt disdain.

Flor de Ceibo sleeps on the lounge chair, which she moves around, following the sun, so tired that she doesn't see a pair of children spying on her from the roof of the house next door. When the sun abandons the garden, she goes back inside and finds her uncle drinking mate and watching the afternoon soap, the one with the worst actors.

"Just like a woman, what do you know..." she murmurs as she passes by.

The uncle is still in his TV-induced stupor. It's time: she drinks skimmed yogurt straight from the pack, downing about a pint without taking a breath. Then she gets into the shower, soaps herself, shaves her legs, buttocks, and crack until they're smooth as a gravestone. She dries herself off. Rubs in cream. The uncle sees her shrouded in a cloud of steam. She puts on the skimpy clothes we saw her wearing that morning.

"Be careful, there are plenty of crazies out there."

"You're telling me... I've got their king right here."

"I mean it. And now to top it all off, the fucking dogs have started crossing the road. There's a crash every other day. The cars flip over trying not to hit the animals. The side of the road is littered in crosses."

"When I need a father, I'll find one that doesn't want to fuck me, you dirty old man."

The uncle stands up, ready to give her a beating, and while her initial reaction is fear, she quickly composes herself and her corrosive smile returns.

"Do it," she goads him. "Do it and see if you ever get a good night's sleep again. I'll burn the fucking house down with you and everything else in it."

As his niece leaves him in the house alone and depressed, watching the soap, his manhood in tatters after his failed attempt at physical abuse, he picks up the towel she used to dry herself and masturbates angrily, squeezing his cock until it spurts a gray, sticky, stinky liquid into the fabric.

III

Flor de Ceibo at work.

A queen surveying her realm of careful drivers. They're afraid of the dogs who've taken to stepping out in front of cars and causing accidents. The animals have grown adept at leading souls into the next world.

Strong legs and hands, capable of strangling a bulky trucker, should the need arise. She begins her night like an actress in a play. She rations her energy. She knows there's no reason to use it all up in the first encounter. She can last all night without having to spend it hanging around the trucks. Summer nights are easy to bear.

"If you're smart, it won't take longer than seven minutes. Just say Yes, papito and grope their package and you'll have them ready to burst. You need to keep an eye on the time. Soon enough, you'll be amazed by how quickly the money rolls in." Advice the travestis gave her when she started out.

Now a pair of johns beckons her over from a car with flashing blue lights, like a police cruiser. She's already seen off one in half an hour and cleaned herself up as best she could in the gas station bathroom. Now she sashays through the night like a snake with hair instead of scales.

Following the requisite negotiations, the three lovers take the car to a motel not far away. It's called the Traveler's Kiss, and it is extremely popular with the local travestis and the few couples who slip away to the remote corner of the planet where this story is set. The boys are simple; they don't say much, they're not curious about her. They talk about the weather, the latest traffic accident: an animal that the specialists haven't yet identified, a kind of dog with long legs, was hit by a car.

Flor de Ceibo is bored, her mind elsewhere, on the nun who waved to her that morning on her way home. The men drone on and on but she's still pondering the nuns' hairy legs and the one bathed in the morning light who smiled so sweetly with drool running down the side of her mouth.

Her eyes fill with tears that she'd never be able to explain to her johns if they asked, so she brings a nail hardened by layer after layer of varnish and flicks them out the car window. The earth burns and vegetation shrivels where they fall.

They get to the motel, settle on a price for the room, get undressed, mess around, and bodies couple and rearrange themselves. Light from the neon arrows pointing the way into the temple of sex by the hour slips through the gaps in the curtain. From her queenly throne, she uses her small but broad foot to stroke the bodies of these farm boys raised on fresh milk and homemade bread while they squeeze her bitch tits, calling her little whore, lovely whore. Flor de Ceibo likes one of them, the younger one. He's tall and well-built. And nice, too. The kind of country bumpkin you want to take away to a cabin in the mountains and force to work the land naked. The kind you want to say "I love you" to while you bite on his peachy nipples. Straight but beautiful.

The other one shoves his cock in her mouth and grabs the back of her head, pushing until she gags, making her feel as though she's fucking a washing machine. Or a chest of drawers.

"Everything all right?" he asks.

"Yes, fine. You don't like how I do it?" Flor de Ceibo asks innocently as though she were thinking about something else entirely. The john's question reminds her this is business. She's picked up a pair of pampas farm boys along the road and now she needs to see to them like the professional she is.

"We'll see. Do it and I'll let you know."

Flor de Ceibo does what she has to do, but she's distracted. What's she doing thinking about those nuns she saw that morning?

It drags on. It looks as though they're going to take a while to come. This could last for hours. Fortunately, the agreed price was by motel hours, so they'll either have to pay up or keep a better eye on the time.

She has some well-proven theories in the field of hurrying orgasms. A girl like her is ready to use every trick in the book. For example, talking to them like a little girl makes them come faster. Baby talk, they call it these days. If she starts to moan and pout, the orgasm comes. It works on a lot of them, and she's honed her technique at getting them hot and bothered. If they're really having trouble, a finger in the ass always tips the balance in her favor. None of her johns struggling to spill their load has been able to resist her finger. A little shuffle and that's it. *Let's see if the theory still holds,* she thinks and wets her middle finger, ready to shove it between the buttocks of the guy she doesn't like so much so she can finish him off quickly and move on to the guy she prefers. It's not mala praxis, but as she proceeds, maybe because her nail is too long, or because she didn't wet her finger enough, when she, concentrating on the blow job, plunges her finger in his ass, the boy hits her in the head, a little above the temple, knocking her over, his face a picture of surprise and indignance.

"Hey, don't hit her," says the other one. "I don't want any trouble with the tranny."

"She tried to shove her finger in my ass, the faggot."

"Don't hit her, or there'll be trouble."

Flor de Ceibo gets back up, still a little dazed. She looks for something to hold on to but can't find anything and falls back down. Finally, she manages to get herself upright and the three of them are silent, sizing each other up as they try to decide what to do next. It's one of those times when you could cut the air with a knife, which is how she plans to describe it to her friends when it's over. The johns are scared when they see Flor de Ceibo sway. You could hear a pin drop. Little by little she steadies herself, and in the blink of an eye, she leaps onto the body that hit her and sinks her teeth into his shoulder. They're a pair of well-built men, but they can't pull her off.

When she lets him go, she sees her johns staring at her in terror. She knows that they need to be afraid of her if she's going to get them to do what she wants.

"Give me your money and his too, plus your cellphones and watch," she says. She reaches into her handbag and takes out a knife that gleams like an ice cube, brandishing it decisively so they know just how dangerous she is.

"Leave me my ID," begs one of the johns.

"I'm giving you back your wallet."

She gets dressed quickly, without taking her eyes off them. She's wet with their saliva; her underwear is damp. And just like that, as if nothing happened, she withdraws from the stage, gracefully, under the worried gazes of the johns who just happened to pick her up that night.

"Wait fifteen minutes before leaving. There are cameras in the room. The motel staff know me. If you try something, they'll defend me."

"We'll meet again," threatens the one she bit.

As she leaves through the motel entrance, she passes one of the cleaning women smoking a cigarette.

"What did you do, Flor?" she asks.

"I didn't do anything."

She takes out a tissue and wipes the blood from her teeth and lips. All that biting messed them up.

When she does these robberies, the adrenaline gets her higher than marijuana; it's better than ecstasy and alcohol. She'd feel guilty, only she's a travesti. She works along the road; guilt isn't for creatures like her. Her lot is to stretch out in the sun, cover herself in Hinds cream and Impulse deodorant, and make her uncle sick with desire. It's to match anyone who attacks her blow for blow, simply, honorably. It's easy to deal with the police. There isn't a policeman alive who doesn't lust for travesti flesh. It's spells, sticking pins into dolls and putting curses on houses. Travestis have done well to sow fear with their spells on the homes of those who abuse them. The gremlin of fear passes from mouth to mouth like a kiss. Flor de Ceibo is protected by the trench she did her part to dig.

IV

Flor de Ceibo walks confidently down the side of the road. She spins like a model on the catwalk when a passing car honks its horn. But the car belonging to the boys she's just robbed swerves off the road and parks on the shoulder in front of her. Flor de Ceibo runs into the fields and disappears among the soybeans.

She runs in her weathered heels, hears people swearing at her from behind, her attackers getting closer. She runs farther and farther into the fields like a fox up to no good, followed by maligned, robbed, and humiliated men. Now it's corn, tall corn, golden like in Flor de Ceibo's dreams, hiding her from pursuers ready to beat the shit out of her for what she did to them, a pair of decent kids who didn't do anything wrong.

The moon is white and pale, and Flor de Ceibo's steely legs start to wobble. She collapses. When the boys see her fall, they approach with caution. While she lies there lifeless on the ground, they decide to search through her handbag to retrieve their cellphones, money, and anything else she might have on her.

"Let's go, we don't want to get caught up in anything," says the short-tempered farm boy.

"We should let someone know," says the other one.

"Leave her for the jackals."

V

Flor de Ceibo opens her eyes. She's in a cool room, so cool she's not hot even under all these blankets and sheets so white they blind your eyes. They smell good. The floor is made of wooden cobbles, and the low ceiling has beams running along it. The room smells good, the walls redolent with whitewash and women's secrets. From the bed, Flor de Ceibo sees a large wooden rosary dangling by her head. One of her eyes hurts; it feels swollen. She brings her hand to her forehead and finds that it's bandaged, swollen all around her eyebrow. The pristine white pillowcase is a relief map of blood, but she can't see that right now.

All she remembers is a few scratches while running through the corn field. She must have bumped her head when she fell. Her hearing begins to return, bringing with it what sounds like a dog panting underneath her bed. She leans over as best she can to check but nothing's there. She can still hear breathing.

The door opens. One of the nuns she saw on the road tip-toes in.

"Are you awake?"

"Where am I?"

"At the convent of the Sisters of Compassion. We found you last night at the end of the garden. We decided not to let anyone know before you woke up, just in case."

The nun leaves and we hear her call down the corridor.

"Sister Rosa! She's woken up!"

Now the barking rings out loud and clear, accompanied by

exclamations of joy from other nuns. The door opens again, and the nun who smiled at her on the road yesterday morning enters. Behind her comes the sound of more nuns' footsteps. A very young, dark-skinned one, as shy as a bunny rabbit, is named Ursula. Another skinny nun, lively as a lizard, curious and sincere, stares at her hardest and introduces herself with a spontaneous kiss on the cheek.

"I'm Shakira."

Flor de Ceibo is a little lost, like she's trying to walk on a waterbed. Did these naughty nuns drug her?

"It's my real name. She was very big when I was born, and my mom loved her. She was fourteen when she had me."

Together with Rosa, Ursula, and Shakira is an old woman they call Mother. They speak to each other in unintelligible whispers. It sounds like another language.

Now Sister Rosa sits down on the edge of the bed. She's so gentle you couldn't possibly be scared of her. She takes her hand, which has a raw scratch on it, and starts to lick it, running her tongue over the wound again and again.

Ursula offers an explanation:

"Saliva is full of antibodies; it'll do you good."

"My name is Sister Rosa. You're at the convent of the Sisters of Compassion. It's November 24, 2019. The doctor has been to see you. We were worried about that terrible bump on your head. You got five stitches. We knew not to call the police, just in case. A lot of girls like you come by here. We've had girls like you stay before—last year and the year before. We hoped that some would take their vows, but none has so far."

After a long pause, patting Flor's hand, she adds:

"You're at home here."

The other nuns giggle a little but Sister Rosa barks, "Be quiet!"

"My uncle must be worried," Flor de Ceibo murmurs.

Blurry images come back to her: nuns feeding her, ghostly nuns washing her, praying at her side, talking to her. Nuns with thick, dirty nails from working in the earth. Sister Rosa lying on the ground, licking her wounded hand. Sleep reclaims her before she can ask any more questions. All she can do is murmur again that they need to let her uncle know.

She wakes up desperate to go to the bathroom. She tries to sit up but she's very weak. Her legs are skin and bone, as though she'd never walked in her life. She feels something uncomfortable under her nightdress. She reaches down and realizes she's wearing a diaper. *Get up, you faggot*, the Flor de Ceibo inside her urges. *Get up, you faggot, come on.* When she does manage to get upright, she can barely last a second. She falls straight back down.

"Girl, what are you doing trying to get up by yourself?! You should have called me."

How can she call her when she can barely open her mouth? It's as though her tongue has grown much too big for her palate; it feels heavy and disobedient. Sister Ursula helps her into the bathroom and pulls down her diaper. Flor de Ceibo is embarrassed to let the nun see her dick, but Ursula doesn't seem to care.

"I need to poop, can you leave?" Flor says, mustering the last of her strength.

"I can't leave you alone in the bathroom. Don't worry, just go. I'll look the other way."

She tries, but her belly refuses to relax.

"I can't."

The nun takes a piece of toilet paper and cleans her penis the way you'd dab at the sides of a baby's mouth. Then she puts the diaper back on and takes her back into the room. The drunken sensation begins to fade.

"I'm a little hungry."

"That's a good sign. A patient who eats is one who survives, as my grandfather used to say. And it's true. We'll bring you some breakfast."

"What time is it?"

"10:13 in the morning. The sun will be coming in through

the window soon. Look." She pulls back the curtain so she can see the sun shining down, the light filtering through the lapacho trees, which are in full bloom.

A little while later we see Flor de Ceibo drinking a deliciously sweet white coffee, served with slices of homemade bread and butter, honey, a bowl of fruit salad, a glass of orange juice, and a lapacho flower on the tray. The bread is spongy and light, the water is cool, and there are slices of ham and cheese on a plate.

"How did you find me?" she asks.

"Thanks to the dog. Nené. Our dog. She came looking for Mother Superior making a fuss; it was early, we were praying the rosary for dawn. We went out and saw Nené sniffing you excitedly and we carried you back."

"I was being chased by a pair of disgruntled customers and ran too far. I didn't realize."

"They were chasing you to beat you up."

"Yes. I robbed them. Their things are in my handbag."

"They must have taken them. All we found in your handbag was your ID and house keys."

Sister Ursula laughs in a way that makes Flor de Ceibo uncomfortable; the sound unsettles her a little. She's heard it before. She remembers documentaries about the African savanna, the hyenas cackling around a dead animal.

Flor de Ceibo continues savoring her coffee, which hasn't yet gone cold.

"You can go back to sleep after your breakfast."

"I think I can walk," says Flor de Ceibo.

She stands up. The nun is very close by. She smells like a damp rag. The nun smiles stupidly, and as she does a line of drool dribbles down and dangles from her chin. She doesn't seem to notice. Flor de Ceibo loses her balance and sits back down.

"I got dizzy."

On her second attempt, leaning on the nun's shoulder, she takes a few steps. These first few steps in the room in the convent are the beginning of a new chapter for her, a change in the nature of her suffering. Soon the doors of the convent will open to her, and she will get to know the layout of the place where she has been cared for.

She walks into a well-lit kitchen with plenty of appliances on the shelves, a wood-fired pizza oven at one end and a gas one at the other. There's a two-door refrigerator and a long table with eight chairs on either side. And then, through another door, a veranda with columns wrapped in ivy and tiny flowers that flutter their yellow petals as though they were alive. And beyond the veranda is a garden with pergolas; damson, peach, apple, and lemon trees; dogs playing; cats sleeping in the branches; and gray birds scattered on the grass like seeds; and behind it all a vegetable patch with its own character, wilder than the Amazon, as healthy and anarchic as anything she's ever seen.

Flor de Ceibo's paces grow steadier. Sister Rosa is harvesting some zucchinis good enough to eat then and there, but when she sees her pass by she smiles again, the same way she smiled on the road that morning. Beyond her, Sister Shakira is feeding the chickens, ducks, and turkeys who strut around like they own the place.

"This is where Nené found you," Sister Rosa tells Flor de Ceibo.

"Is she a nun?" she asks, a little disoriented from the walk and all these dream-like visions. She thought she saw the oldest nun, the Mother Superior, milking a goat that bleated between each squeeze.

"No, she's our dog," answers Sister Shakira. "Nené! Come here, Nené!"

She hears a good-sized animal shaking herself off in the undergrowth, the moan of a bitch woken early from her nap, and the heavy padding of paws. A little while later a muzzle appears in the low grass, strong, square, and dun-colored, followed by horse-like haunches. She's tall and dignified. Flor de Ceibo gets a fright when she sees her and falls back onto the soft grass. Nené comes over, sniffs her, and for a second Flor de Ceibo Argañaraz thinks she sees her smile.

"Don't be afraid, she's harmless," says Sister Shakira.

Noise comes from the convent veranda. Flor de Ceibo stands up to see what's going on, and past the plants and animals she sees a pair of nuns on the floor, pulling each other's hair, fighting like ordinary layfolk. They aren't wearing anything beneath their habits. Just hair and a dark thicket around the pubis. They're separated by the oldest nun, the one they call Mother. She smacks them apart with a rod, shouting for good measure.

Flor de Ceibo can't breathe; she doesn't blink or move a muscle. Nené is close by. Her ferocious-looking muzzle is an inch from her nose. The little nun with the flighty habit has told her that she's a dog, but this isn't a dog. It's something else. It's like it can read her thoughts. Nené steps back and howls like a witch. Then she sneezes and runs off excitedly to chase the chickens around the garden.

"Oh my goodness! What is that?" Flor de Ceibo exclaims.

"They wanted to kill her. We tempted her here with food. She had a brother, but he was killed by a farmer," says the Mother Superior on her return from breaking up the fight.

"She's pregnant, you know," she goes on, helping Flor to her feet with an ease that belies her years. Heroic strength. "People don't know what's good for them. They've started to hate them because they say they're satanic. But I say how can a satanic animal be happy living in a convent? We have to keep her from drinking the holy water."

"She was barking at my knees, trying to warn me something was going on," adds Sister Rosa. "She's smart. We need to understand her better, but it's almost like how we talk to each other. She stayed by your door all night. When it's hot she likes to sleep inside or out here in the woods."

"Are you tired?" Shakira asks.

"A little, but I'd like to stay out in the sun," says Flor de Ceibo.

Midday comes around, and for lunch they have sandwiches of homemade goat's cheese, tomatoes from the garden, and fried eggs. The bread is spread with avocado, also from the garden. It's clear that God loves this convent.

As they enjoy the food, accompanied by lemonade, they hear a crash on the road, several hundred feet away. Sisters Ursula and Shakira leave the table and run off to see what happened.

"Nené," says Sister Rosa, jumping up from her chair. "Please, finish your lunch. We need to see what happened."

She goes off calling "Nené, Nené," but the dog, or whatever it is, doesn't come.

"We're always on tenterhooks," says the Mother Superior. "She's a lovely animal but people don't like her. The farmers are superstitious, as you probably know. They see them in the fields and start shooting because they're scared. A vet came once and said that they're not domesticated. He told me the name, but I've forgotten. But I can prove to you that they're perfectly tame."

The Mother Superior gets up easily and beckons to Flor de Ceibo, who's very much enjoying her sandwich. "Come with me."

They walk down a cool, clean passage to an ordinary looking door. The Mother Superior opens it and what appears before Flor de Ceibo's eyes is a garden very different from the one she was in that morning. This one is even bigger, with fewer trees but plenty of roses, and carnivorous angel's-trumpets ready to snap up a hummingbird in the blink of an eye. Leaping around everywhere are hundreds of dogs like Nené. Hundreds of dogs with horse hooves. They gambol around Flor de Ceibo's legs, threatening to knock her over, but the Mother Superior holds her up with her freakish strength.

"If we don't keep them here, they'll die out," says the Mother Superior as she laughs and coos to the animals, who are happy to see her. "Come on, let's finish our lunch. Tomorrow, if you like, I'll introduce you to them all. They're baptized. I did it myself in the chapel font. If the priest ever finds out, he'll kill me."

They go back to the dining room and finish eating. A little while later, Sisters Ursula, Shakira, and Rosa return with sorrowful expressions. Shakira can't stop spinning around, like she's momentarily lost her mind.

"Nené again... She stood in front of a car and it swerved into a milk truck."

"Were there fatalities?" asks the Mother Superior wearily.

"The family in the car. A couple with a little girl."

Flor de Ceibo immediately thinks of Magda, the girl she spoke to in the gas station. Ursula resumes her lunch, lost in thought.

"Do you know the names of the victims?"

"No. It was a red Ford Ka. It got destroyed."

"What about Nené?"

"We don't know. She ran off across the road. So they said."

"She's alive, otherwise the others would be going nuts," says Sister Shakira.

They take Flor de Ceibo back to her room and let her rest all afternoon. At night, they bring her dinner: vegetable soup with half an avocado in it, sprinkled with lemon juice. To drink there's cold green tea. It's brought by Sister Rosa.

"There's no way we can let you leave."

"Of course you can. I can leave whenever I want," says Flor de Ceibo, emboldened by the food.

"You can't. Nené asked us to keep you. You can't leave."

Flor de Ceibo suspects that they're drugging her food. She knocks the tray to the floor and shoves the nun with the maternal smile over a small stool by an antique wooden desk. When she opens the door, the enormous dogs are there, staring at Sister Rosa, who gets back up, laughing and groaning.

Flor de Ceibo tries to leave but the dogs growl at her, the hair on their flanks bristling. She senses that this isn't something that she'll be able to handle tonight. Sister Rosa's insanely dangerous smile is as bright as the neon sign outside the sinful motel. She goes back to bed and surrenders to sleep while the nun clears away the tray and food.

VI

She keeps asking to speak to her uncle, but the nuns keep coming up with excuses. They sound convincing at the time. It's all she can do to stagger to the bathroom; she doesn't have the strength to resist right now. She wakes up at night determined to find a phone. She's heard one ringing—it must be nearby—but even when there isn't a pack of dogs sitting outside her door, the dizziness sends her back to bed.

One morning, she reaches the door to the garden with the dogs and sees her uncle being ripped apart by the beasts. *I hope it's the drugs*, prays Flor de Ceibo as she approaches the carnage. *Let it be the drugs, the drugs.* But it's her uncle, the skinny face, the sunken eyes, the stubble yellowed by tobacco. The dogs growl at each other, jostling to rip a piece of flesh off the body. A hand takes her by the hair and forces her down on her knees. When she looks behind her, she sees the outline of the Mother Superior completely naked. She doesn't have a single hair on her body.

"I told you that your uncle wasn't answering the phone. Now you know why. He hurt you very badly, Flor de Ceibo. He deserved it. The dogs are just."

VII

On nights of the waning moon, the nuns take a naked Flor de Ceibo out to the second garden, the huge garden patrolled by the dogs. They lay her down on a stone in the night air and draw an inverted cross on her forehead with blood from the Mother Superior's hand. Regardless of the weather. They call Nené, who trots over. The dogs lie down, howling while the nuns perform the ritual. They sing Christian hymns:

> God is here today, as certain as the air I breathe,
> as certain as the rising sun,
> as certain as when I sing you'll hear my song.

Nené jumps onto the stone, stands over Flor de Ceibo's body, and licks her from head to toe with her sandpaper tongue. It tickles Flor de Ceibo terribly, but she's usually numb from the nuns' homemade wine. They drink like there's no tomorrow before every ritual. She goes happily every time, without a hint of resignation. They treat her like a queen, like a movie star. There, in the night on the sacrificial stone, Nené kisses her all over, her front, her back, every inch. The nuns play the tambourine and sing. She laughs up at the waning moon and lets them. Then, amid hallelujahs and dog stink, she sees Nené stand up and slowly turn into her. Flor de Ceibo. The same hair, the same skin, the same eyes. The Mother Superior hands her the clothes they found her wearing in the corn field and lovingly helps the new Flor de Ceibo into them.

Every night of the waning moon, Flor de Ceibo Argañaraz sees herself leave the second garden while the nuns sing. She goes straight out to the road. She'd like to warn her johns that it's not her, it's a dog with horse hooves that causes accidents on the road, just for the fun of it. But she doesn't have the strength to follow Nené, her usurper. She'll escape someday, when she finds out what kind of order the Sisters of Compassion is and how you get out of there. But it's hard for her to summon the energy: the food is very good and the sheets smell lovely.

Contributors

Maximiliano Barrientos was born in Santa Cruz de la Sierra, Bolivia, in 1979. He is a teacher and the author of the short-story collections *Diario* (2009), *Fotos tuyas cuando empiezas a envejecer* (2011), and *Una casa en llamas* (2015) and the novels *Hoteles* (2011, translated into Portuguese), *La desaparición del paisaje* (2015), *En el cuerpo una voz* (2018), and *Miles de ojos* (2021).

Sarah Booker is an educator and literary translator. Her translations include Mónica Ojeda's *Jawbone*; Gabriela Ponce's *Blood Red*; and Cristina Rivera Garza's *New and Selected Stories*, *Grieving: Dispatches from a Wounded Country*, and *The Iliac Crest*. She has a PhD in Hispanic Literature from UNC-Chapel Hill and is currently based in Morganton, North Carolina, where she teaches Spanish at the North Carolina School of Science and Mathematics.

Lisa Dillman is translator of some thirty novels, including those by Yuri Herrera, Pilar Quintana, Alejandra Costamagna, Andrés Barba, Sabina Berman, and Eduardo Halfon. She lives in Atlanta, Georgia, and teaches in the Department of Spanish and Portuguese at Emory University.

Tomás Downey (Buenos Aires, Argentina, 1984) is a translator and screenwriter and one of the foremost short-story writers in Argentina today. His work tends to draw out the strangeness hidden beneath the surface of everyday life. He is the author of three short-story collections: *Acá el tiempo es otra cosa*, *El lugar donde mueren los pájaros*, and *Flores que se abren de noche*.

Mariana Enriquez is a writer and journalist based in Buenos Aires. She is the author of the novel *Our Share of Night* as well as two short-story collections, *Things We Lost in the Fire* and *The Dangers of Smoking in Bed*, all three translated by Megan McDowell. *The Dangers of Smoking in Bed* was a finalist for the International Booker Prize; the Kirkus Prize; the Ray Bradbury Prize for Science Fiction, Fantasy, & Speculative Fiction; and the *Los Angeles Times* Book Prize in Fiction.

Joaquín Gavilano is a Bolivian translator, poet, and MFA candidate in creative writing and translation at the University of Arkansas. Joaquín currently serves as a translation editor for *The Arkansas International*. He is the recipient of a 2023 PEN/Heim Translation fund grant and the Carolyn F. Walton Cole First-Year Fellowship in translation from the University of Arkansas.

Lina Munar Guevara (b. 1996) is a writer and lawyer from Bogotá, Colombia. Her novel *Imagina que rompes todo* [Imagine breaking everything] was published by Himpar Editores in 2022. She has written stories for Colombia Diversa based on testimonies from LGBTQI victims of the Colombian armed conflict and has worked as a translator for the Colombian Truth Commission and the International Institute of Humanitarian Law in San Remo. She has an MFA in creative writing from New York University.

Tim Gutteridge is a creative translator based in Edinburgh, Scotland. He translates literary fiction and nonfiction, theater, and texts for the Spanish audiovisual and publishing sectors. His translations include *The Hand That Feeds You* by Mercedes Rosende (Bitter Lemon), *The Cook of Castamar* by Fernando Muñez (Head of Zeus), *The Mountain That Eats Men* by Ander Izagirre (Zed Books), and *The Swallow* by Guillem Clua (Cervantes Theatre, London).

Claudia Hernández is the highly acclaimed author of five short-story collections and three novels, the first of which was *Slash and Burn*, published in Spanish in 2017 and in English (in Julia Sanches' translation) in 2020. Her work has appeared in various anthologies in Spain, Italy, France, Germany, Israel, and the U.S.A.

Julian Isaza (b. 1979) is a Colombian writer and journalist. His works of fiction and nonfiction have won national and international prizes. He has published two collections of horror and science fiction stories to date.

Ellen Jones is a writer, editor, and literary translator from Spanish. Her recent and forthcoming translations include *Cubanthropy* by Iván de la Nuez (Seven Stories Press, 2023), *The Remains* by Margo Glantz (Charco Press, 2023), and *Nancy* by Bruno Lloret (Two Lines Press, 2021). Her monograph, *Literature in Motion: Translating Multilingualism Across the Americas*, was published by Columbia University Press (2022). Her short fiction has appeared in *The London Magazine* and *Slug*.

Kit Maude is a translator based in Buenos Aires. He has translated dozens of Latin American writers for a wide array of publications and writes reviews for *Ñ*, *Otra Parte*, and the *Times Literary Supplement*.

Megan McDowell has translated many of the most important Latin American writers working today. Her translations have won the National Book Award for Translated Literature, the English PEN award, the Premio Valle-Inclán, and two O. Henry Prizes and have been nominated for the International Booker

Prize (four times) and the Kirkus Prize. Her short-story translations have been featured in *The New Yorker*, *The Paris Review*, *The New York Times Magazine*, *Tin House*, *McSweeney's*, and *Granta*, among others. In 2020 she won an Award in Literature from the American Academy of Arts and Letters. She is from Richmond, Kentucky, and lives in Santiago, Chile.

Sarah Moses is a Canadian writer and translator from Spanish and French. Her translations include titles by Argentine authors such as Agustina Bazterrica, Ariana Harwicz, Alberto Manguel, and Paula Rodríguez. With Tomás Downey, she co-translated *Sos una sola persona* by Canadian poet Stuart Ross. Her own writing has appeared in Spanish and English in the chapbooks *as they say* and *Those Problems*.

Mónica Ojeda (Ecuador, 1988) is the author of the novels *La desfiguración Silva*, *Nefando*, and *Mandíbula*, as well as the poetry collections *El ciclo de las piedras* and *Historia de la leche*. Her stories have been published in the anthology *Emergencias: Doce cuentos iberoamericanos* and the collections *Caninos* and *Las voladoras*. In 2017, she was included on the Bógota39 list of the best thirty-nine Latin American writers under forty, and in 2019, she received the Prince Claus Next Generation Award in honor of her outstanding literary achievements.

Antonio Diaz Oliva (ADO) has published five books in Spanish, including the novel *Campus* (Chatos Inhumanos, NYC), a tragi-comic and absurdist satire of the power dynamics among Latin American academics at U.S. universities. He received the Roberto Bolaño Young Writers Award and the National Book Award for Best Story Collection in Chile. He lives in Chicago, where he works as an editor at the Museum of Contemporary Art. "Rabbits" is part of *Gente un poco dañada*, a short-story collection that explores the weird and the eerie.

Noelle de la Paz is a writer and literary translator. Her work appears in *The Recluse, Southwest Review, Kenyon Review*, and elsewhere, and in the exhibitions *Otherwise Obscured: Erasure in Body and Text* (Franklin Street Works) and *Boulevard of Ghosts* (Local Project). She was a 2021/22 Emerge–Surface–Be Fellow at The Poetry Project and has also received support from Brooklyn Poets and the Queens Council for the Arts.

Giovanna Rivero is a Bolivian writer born in Montero, Santa Cruz. Her publications include the short-story collections *Para comerte mejor* and *Tierra fresca de su tumba*, as well as the novel *98 segundos sin sombra*. In 2004, she took part in the Iowa Writing Program at the University of Iowa, and in 2006 she was awarded a Fulbright grant. In 2011, she was named one of "the 25 Best-Kept Literary Secrets of Latin America" by Mexico's Guadalajara International Book Fair.

Julia Sanches translates literature from Catalan, Spanish, and Portuguese into English.

Camila Sosa Villada was born in 1982 in La Falda (Córdoba, Argentina). She is a writer, actress, and singer and previously earned a living as a sex worker, street vendor, and hourly maid. She holds degrees in communication and theater from the National University of Córdoba. Her first novel, *Bad Girls* (published as *The Queens of Sarmiento Park* in the UK), won the Premio Sor Juana Inés de la Cruz and the Grand Prix de l'Héroïne Madame Figaro and will be translated into seventeen languages. *I'm a Fool to Want You*, from which this story is taken, will be published in spring 2024.

Joel Streicker's fiction has been published widely and recently won *Cutthroat Magazine*'s and *Blood Orange Review*'s short-story contests. Streicker is the author of the poetry collection *El amor en los tiempos de Belisario*. His translations of such writers as Samanta Schweblin, Mariana Enriquez, and Pilar Quintana have appeared in *A Public Space*, *McSweeney's*, and other journals. Streicker's essays have appeared in *American Ethnologist*,

The Forward, and *Boletín cultural y bibliográfico*, among other publications.

Johanna Warren is a singer/songwriter and interdisciplinary artist based in rural Wales. She was the recipient of a 2013 NEA literary translation fellowship and is currently writing a TV series and scoring a new musical adaptation of Euripides' *The Bacchae*.

CALICO

The Calico Series, published biannually by
Two Lines Press, captures vanguard works
of translated literature in stylish, collectible
editions. Each Calico is a vibrant snapshot
that explores one aspect of our present
moment, offering the voices of previously
inaccessible, highly innovative writers from
around the world today.